RETALIATE

kristin harte

RETALIATE

kristin harte

Chapter One

BISHOP

Hit me."

I shot my best friend Gage a grin, the same one I tended to use when I was about to close a deal. The one my older brother called my salesman smile. "You sure you want to do that?"

Gage stared me down, his almost-black eyes giving nothing away. "Hit me, jackass."

Shaking my head slowly, I clucked and frowned. "You'll bust."

"You trying to play this game for me?"

"Nope. Just looking out for you."

He squinted, trying hard to make me crack. But I wasn't about to hang myself with the rope he fed me. I waited him out, sitting deep in my seat. Casual and confident. And bluffing like a motherfucker to throw him off his game. The guy had luck to spare when he played cards, and I hated to lose.

Gage clenched his jaw. "Hit me."

I tossed his fifth card across the table, noting what he already showed. A spread made up of two threes, a five, and a four. Fifteen on the way to not pass twenty-one. No way did he not go over with the new card.

"Either you just busted, or you've got yourself a five card Charlie hand. I'm going to go with the first option. I stand."

Gage flipped the card over, giving me no tell as to whether he'd gotten a good one or a bad one. And then he laid it down.

Six of hearts. Twenty-one on a five-card spread.

"Motherfucker." I picked up my own cards—totaling just eighteen—and waggled my fingers for his.

"You're a sore loser," he noted as he handed over his cards.

"Am not." Okay, that might have come out a little more petulant than I'd intended. "I'm just not used to losing is all. It's such a rarity for me."

Gage snorted. "Keep telling yourself that."

"Bishop trying to pull that 'I never lose' line again?" Deacon, owner of the bar we'd decided to play blackjack in, set a plate of Buffalo wings in front of us and dropped into an empty chair. "He's been trying that crap since the day I met him."

Gage might have smiled—hard to tell considering the impressive beard the man sported. "He's been trying that crap since the day *I* met him, and that was a hell of a lot earlier than you did."

"So you're saying he's been a sore loser for a long time?"

"Fuck off," I said, tossing a napkin at Deacon.

Gage wasn't about to be deterred. "I need to know how far back this inability to lose goes. Where's Alder tonight?"

Deacon nearly choked on his beer. "Dude's been drooling over Shye for three damn long years and finally managed to convince that little blonde to give him the time of day. Where do you *think* he is?"

No way was I arguing that. "If the man isn't face, finger, or cock deep right now, he's doing life wrong."

Deacon raised his eyebrows...and his beer. "Cheers to that."

Gage looked as if he wanted to reply, but his phone lighting up distracted him. He tapped the screen a few times then ran his finger along the edge, scrolling. The more he read, the more the furrows in his brow deepened. I'd have bet money he was frowning under all that dark hair.

"Problem?" I asked before taking a long, deep pull from my beer.

Deacon gave me a smirk. "It's late. That's either a booty call, or someone's drunk and needs a ride home."

"If they're drunk, that means they're buying their liquor someplace other than your bar," I replied.

Deacon shrugged, looking around at the almost-empty bar. The Jury Room was busier than it should be for a Tuesday night but not packed. "If they want to waste their money on the well liquor and warm beer over at Tracks in Rock Falls, that's their own problem."

Tracks was the only other bar within a forty-mile radius of Justice, the tiny town where I'd been raised and where I still lived. It was a shithole, too, which made Deacon's place the crown jewel of the area. Not that it was all that nice. Dive bar definitely described the place, but the food was good and the beer was cold. What more did anyone need?

Gage finally looked away from his phone. "We've got a problem."

"Shit." Deacon set his beer down and leaned in. Ready and focused. Looking so much like my brother Alder in that moment. "Sheriff Baker nosing around town again, or is it the Soul Suckers?"

Gage grunted, focused on his phone again. His thumbs flying over the screen. "Hang on."

Oh sure, right. We should just *hang on*. As if either option Deacon mentioned could simply be set aside so he could send emojis to whoever was on the other end of the conversation. The Soul Suckers motorcycle club had caused a fuckton of trouble over the past couple of weeks. The sort of trouble that led to burned-down houses and a funeral for a friend's wife. My brother Alder's new girl had been at the center of the first wave of attacks, which had all stemmed from a meth lab the club had been running in our woods. They'd sent their guys to take out Alder after we'd cut them off from their drug kitchen—men who never made it back home. Not that anyone other than those of us who'd handled the situation knew anything about that. Gage, Alder, and I had made sure those men could never tell the tale of their demise.

The motorcycle club had to assume we'd killed them, yet it'd been quiet for a couple of weeks in town. Too quiet. And Sheriff Baker...well, he was crooked as fuck. Always had been. If he caught wind of what we'd done, we'd likely go to jail. Not nearly as bad as what the Soul Suckers would do to us, but not good either.

"I can't believe they haven't hit us already," I said as I spun my beer bottle, my mind whirling faster than the glass. "Two of their club brothers never made it home. If they were my guys—"

"We'd go after them right away." Gage—current heavy machinery mechanic for my family's logging business, Kennard Mills, and my former SEAL teammate—seemed to be on the same wavelength. Not surprising. "You and me, we'd bust through their doors and take their team down before they got their bearings. Alder and Deacon here wouldn't."

Deacon grabbed a wing and bit into it before throwing out an extended, sarcastic-sounding, "Nope."

They weren't wrong. That was a huge difference in how my older brother and I handled conflicts—as SEALs, Gage and I powered in and did what was needed. As Green Berets, my brother and Deacon plotted and planned, looked at every angle before deciding on the best course of action. SEALs were direct—Green Berets were sneaky as fuck. The Soul Suckers were being sneaky. I'd bet my life on it.

"Let's double up on security at the ridge." I cracked my neck, trying to think like my older brother. "Alder would rely on sabotage to throw the enemy off, which means the Soul Suckers might as well. We don't need anyone coming in to fuck with our equipment."

"Already on it, though that brings us to another issue. The texts I just got."

"Your booty call?" Deacon asked, waggling his eyebrows in the most ridiculous way.

"If that was a booty call text, he'd be out the door already. Not sitting here with me, Deac."

Deacon shrugged. "Maybe he likes your smile more than hers, pretty boy."

I pulled out my best grin for that one. "I am quite popular."

Gage just rolled his eyes. "You two know Felicia in Rock Falls?"

Sure did. As did every other man who worked at Kennard Mills. Felicia had been the topic of conversation since she'd moved to the area a few months back. She'd flirted hard and had made a few obvious moves to get my attention, but there was no way. I didn't fuck close to home—too easy to fall into a mess of clinginess and a woman wanting more than I was willing to offer. And I was definitely not interested in more *or* her.

Deacon grinned. "Tall, legs for days, sweetest little swing to her ass when she walks around the liquor store where she works. Yeah, I know her. That's your booty call? I figured Bishop would be hitting that. Seems more his type."

True, she had a look every man would go for, but she had one thing I avoided.

Before I could say a word, Gage shook his head. "Bishop doesn't mess with redheads."

Deacon sat back, obviously stunned. "Why the hell not?"

Both men looked at me expectantly, but there was no way I was heading down that path. "I prefer blondes. What's Felicia texting you about?"

"The weather."

I blinked, searching my mind for the euphemism in that answer. I didn't find it.

Deacon must not have either. "The hot redhead working at the liquor store is texting you about the weather? Man, and Bishop said *Alder* might be doing life wrong."

"Shut up, old man," Gage said without a bit of anger in his voice. "The chick's got a degree in meteorology and has been watching the forecast models for the past two weeks. Our rainy season is about to get worse."

That definitely caught my attention. Wood ruled my life. Always had, always would. Growing up the son of a sawmill owner, I had no choice. The obsession with growth rates, species diversity, and forestry just sort of happened. I'd been out in the woods with my dad as a child, had learned to detect the healthy trees from the ones that needed to be culled by the time I'd started playing peewee football. Like every logger's child, I'd learned geometry calculating stumpage, the amount of board feet possible based on the diameter of a tree trunk at chest height. Of course, at that age, it'd been at a height over my head, but my dad had made sure I could figure out the calculations. Trees and lumber had become my *thing*. Weather came in at a close second, though. Especially bad weather.

And in a Rocky Mountain Front rainy season, there was only one kind of bad weather. "That cold front moving up the range is going to stall right on top of us, isn't it?"

"Looks like it." Gage took another drink of his beer, killing the bottle. "She told me at least a week of solid rain, likely starting tomorrow afternoon."

Fuck, that wasn't good. "Looks like we're going to get wet, boys."

Deacon snorted. "It's going to rain. Whatever. Let's get back to the more important question of why Felicia isn't getting wet from either one of you."

Gage shrugged, picking up his phone and typing out a message. "I'm not interested."

The former Special Forces sniper across the table just shook his head disbelievingly. "And, Bishop? No redheads? What's the matter with gingers?"

Still not going there. "I'd rather know why you're not the one hitting that if you think she's so perfect."

Deacon balked. "That girl is half my age."

I did the math—Deacon seemed to be about as old as my brother, Alder. Felicia looked to be about as old as my youngest sibling, Lainie. That made him a lot less than twice her age. "No way. She's maybe a decade younger."

The look he shot me held a hell of a lot of sarcasm. "Not much better, man."

Gage grabbed a chicken wing, finally ignoring his phone for a minute. "So Bishop doesn't date redheads—"

"Keep the D-word to yourself," I interrupted.

Gage was not to be deterred, apparently. "Fine. Bishop doesn't date at all, and he doesn't *do* redheads. Deacon doesn't like women too much younger than him. That right?"

Deacon sat back with a grin. "I'm waiting for some rich cougar to come sweep me off my feet."

"You're going to be waiting a long damn time," I said.

"Nah. I went to a psychic when I was in Vegas last time. She said I'd find my soul mate before the end of the year."

My chest tightened. Vegas psychic hit all of my *fuck no* buttons, not because I didn't think some of them had talents. No, I knew some did. One in particular. The one who was the reason I never messed with redheaded women.

Gage stared across the table. "You went to a psychic?"

"Yeah. Cute little thing—all blond and big-eyed. Great rack too." He held out his hands as if cupping said breasts, making Gage laugh as I grabbed my bottle and took another swig. Trying to force down the sick rising in my gut.

Not her, not her. Blond not red. Can't be her.

"So were you trying to find out about your future or get a date?" Gage asked.

"Definitely a date. Which I would have gotten, but then she saw the soul mate thing and said she couldn't poach another woman's man so close to us meeting."

"Wait," Gage said, holding up his hand. "You got cock-blocked by your own future?"

I choked on my beer.

Deacon scowled. "Fuck off."

Gage's laugh exploded, drawing the attention of the few bar patrons sitting around. It even made his dog Rex get up out of the little bed Deacon kept by the door for him and come padding over. We'd never had a pet growing up—with five kids, I always figured my mom and dad had enough to deal with—so Rex and I had tenuous sort of relationship. One that had not been strengthened when he and his owner had moved in with me a few months back. But Gage loved the hairy little fucker. As did Deacon, though he'd never come right out and say it.

Still, the dog made for the perfect distraction.

"C'mon, Rex," Deacon said, pushing to his feet. "Let's go see what kind of treats I have for you in the back and leave these two dumbasses to their cards."

No way was I letting an opportunity pass. "Watch out, man. You might miss your soul mate if you disappear for too long."

Deacon flipped me off as he headed to the back. I considered that a win.

"He can't believe that bullshit," Gage said, shaking his head.

"You don't buy it?"

"Psychics and future-telling and stuff?" He frowned. "Not a bit. You do?"

I shrugged, trying hard not to think about tarot cards and tea leaves and all the things I'd been completely surrounded by at one time. "I think some people are more intuitive than others."

"Well, I think some people are more devious than others and know how to manipulate people into giving up just enough information to feed their lies."

"Remind me to take you to meet Miss Hansen one of these days. You might change your mind."

"The old lady up on Widow's Ridge?"

"Yeah. She's psychic—used to read tea leaves and tarot and shit."

He grunted. "Some old lady with a good sense of people isn't going to change my mind."

It wouldn't have changed mine either. But then her granddaughter had moved in with her, and I'd learned firsthand how the talent Miss Hansen displayed had transferred down through the generations. But Gage didn't know about Anabeth Monroe—Vegas performer and famous tarot card reader—and if I had my way, he never would.

"Come on," I said, grabbing the cards and shuffling the deck. "Let's play another round or two."

"You going to pout when you lose again?"

I grinned, clinging to the distraction with every fiber of my being. "You're assuming I'm going to lose. I told you, it's a rarity for me."

Unless we were talking about women. About me losing my heart and soul to the fiery redhead who'd walked away without a word of explanation. The one I'd never really gotten over. The one I occasionally saw on pop culture news reports even though I tried to avoid anything having to do with her.

I sucked at romance, apparently, but I could play cards. And I wouldn't lose again.

"Hey, Deacon," I yelled, catching the owner's attention when he came out of the kitchen. "Two more beers over here. I've got a long night of winning ahead of me."

Chapter Two

ANABETH

The sky had darkened gradually over the two days I'd been in Justice, the typical late-summer clouds building above us. On my third morning in town, the rain seemed to be ready to fall at any moment. As were my tears.

Don't cry. Don't cry. Whatever you do, you're not allowed to cry.

The chants echoed in my head, not really soothing anything but giving me something to focus on. For two days, sheer will had been the only thing keeping me from sobbing my eyes out every time I left my grandma alone in her room. I wouldn't have left her at all today seeing as how the end seemed to be barreling toward us, but I'd needed the comfort of a good cup of tea. So I'd screwed up the courage to walk out her bedroom door, then I'd headed for my favorite room in the big old farmhouse where she'd spent most of her life... And where she would soon die.

The wood floors of her kitchen gleamed beneath my feet, and the cream-colored cabinets practically sparkled. All looking the same as when I'd first moved in to this house as a preteen girl with a chip on my shoulder from too many years in foster care. But the spot that had always called to me, the one I had loved from the second I'd seen it, was the window seat. Big and deep, that padded nook was one I could curl up in for hours on an overcast day like this one, tea in one hand, book in the other. All things I'd learned to love because of spending time with my grandmother, Miss "don't call me Missy or Melissa, it's just Miss" Hansen.

But I wasn't sitting today, wasn't reading either. I was preparing to grieve the one person in this world who had ever truly cared about me...well, the only one I hadn't destroyed.

As the water heated, I pulled my beloved tarot deck from my pocket. The one Miss had bought me at a strange little store in Rock Falls, long since closed. The deck had fallen into our cart twice, had practically burned my hand the first time I'd touched it. All things Miss had said indicated we were meant to be together.

The deck never left my side, had been my constant companion for almost two decades. The cards had stood the test of time, though —no fading or rips, just a slight patina from so much use and a softness to the edges that spoke of being shuffled and pulled too many times to count.

More habitual than intentional, I shuffled the cards, spinning and weaving the deck in my hands until it finally felt right. Felt like it was ready for me. I flipped the top card over. A heart pierced by three swords floated in the middle, the background showing a gray and rainy sky. Simple, easy to understand—the three of swords meant a grim moment in time and brought with it grief and sorrow.

I'd pulled it nearly every day since I'd left Justice all those years ago.

"The cards never lie," I whispered, telling myself the same thing I told all my customers. The ones who came to me with big smiles and anxious eyes. The ones hoping to be told something positive, something they could look forward to. I never read them the three of swords—never told them what that card meant if it appeared for them. I let them have their hopeful future, instead. But me? I knew too much. There was no hiding from what I'd been through...and what was coming my way.

With shaky hands and a sick stomach, I slid the card into the pile and tucked the deck back into my pocket. Better not to think about it any more than I had to.

When the kettle whistled, I grabbed the little tin of spearmint tea off the counter. Almost empty—it had been full when I'd arrived, which meant my tea obsession had gotten a little out of hand. I had a second container, but at the rate I was going, that'd be gone in a matter of days. Easy fix in Vegas, where I could have almost anything I desired shipped right to me. Out here in Justice? Up on Widow's Ridge? That wasn't happening. Even the post office, where I normally would have sent a package, wasn't an option. If word got out that I was back, if certain people figured out I was home... Well, that would end badly. For all of us, but especially me. And I simply didn't have it in me to lose my only family and deal with past mistakes.

One heartbreak at a time.

Water in my cup and tea steeping, I headed back to the little bedroom on the east side of the house. Miss had always liked waking up with the sun rising over the mountain. She used to say the golden light warming her skin was much like the kiss of a lover so early in the day. I used to blush and grow embarrassed by that sort of talk, but I'd grown up as we were all supposed to do. I'd learned that her words were not sexual in nature but intimate.

I'd grown to love that first kiss of light almost as much as she had since that was the only time I allowed myself to remember what it felt like to wake up warm, loved, and in the arms of a man my heart beat for. I gave myself those few minutes every day to remember, and then I would slam the door on those memories and force myself back to reality. Wishes and dreams and regrets would never pay the bills, and being sorry didn't guarantee forgiveness.

As I walked through the door and saw Miss lying in the bed, my current reality hit me so hard, I nearly lost my breath. Pale and weak, frail in appearance, Miss stole every ounce of my attention. Shallow breaths caused the sheet to move, but otherwise, she lay still. Almost silent. Almost gone. The end was close—I could feel the cold tentacles of death creeping closer with every moment. Could sense her ferocious spirit leaving, her presence fading from the world we knew as the end approached. I doubted she had more than a morning or two left on this earth.

"Hey, Miss." I settled into the chair beside her bed and reached for her hand. Needing to savor our connection while I could. "I'm running low on my tea. I'm sure you know how much of a tragedy that is for me."

No answer, no response—not that I'd expected one. She'd slipped into what I could only assume was a coma early that morning. I'd already called hospice to come help me with final care, but they didn't have anyone in the area at the moment, so it was just Miss and me. Exactly as it had been for so many years. Before I'd screwed up too big to stay in Justice and deal with the fallout from my actions.

"I'd have some sent to me, but then I'd need to go to the post office. I don't think letting people know I'm back would be a good idea right now." I glanced down into my tea, watching the leaves float, wondering what I'd see once they settled. Terrified to find out. "Remember the summer you taught me to read tea leaves? You said I needed to know more than the cards, so you made that my project while I didn't have school. We sat outside every day for hours, drinking tea and waiting for the future to show itself." I blew on my cup, the golden ripples agitating the leaves on the bottom. Moving them around. Changing the future for just a moment before the dark spots settled once more. "I didn't even like tea then, but you didn't care. You just kept trying new ones until we found one I could tolerate."

So many good memories. So many bad ones too. Because the summer Miss taught me to read the shapes and patterns left behind in the leaves was the same one I met the Kennard boys. When I met Bishop.

I looked up, unable not to notice the picture on the bookshelf across from the bed. Over a decade before, Miss had framed a silly shot of Bishop and me hugging before the homecoming dance my senior year. She'd never taken it down. Not even when I'd asked her to. Not even when I'd cried and begged and threatened never to come back to Justice if I had to see it. As always, Miss had known best—the picture that had at one time sliced through my chest and made me bleed now gave me comfort. Something I so desperately needed.

"I guess I could have a shipment sent to the mill. I could call him and ask if anyone there would mind. I bet Alder would make sure anything we sent there got to us." Alder, the oldest Kennard brother. Not Bishop. I had a feeling if Bishop saw my name on a package, he'd throw the box in the trash, and I'd deserve that for what I did to him. Which was why I'd never looked back once I'd left Justice...until last week.

But I'd only come home for one reason—to take care of Miss in her final days. The cancer eating away at her brain and bones had taken its time showing up, but once it had, the end seemed to appear out of nowhere. And just like the life I'd been living for the past fourteen years, all hope had been exhausted with a single doctor's appointment. Her oncologist had told her there was no more he could do, no more options for treatment or care—it was time to get her affairs in order and say goodbye.

Miss had headed straight home and called me to let me know the end was coming, something I'd already seen in the cards I pulled every day. Something I'd been preparing for since the day she'd called to tell me they'd found a shadow on an X-ray. Something I'd been dreading and trying so very hard not to think about.

That last phone call—when she'd said she didn't want to die alone, that it was time for me to come home—had been the only thing that could have gotten me to come back. I'd refused to miss her final days or to leave her to pass without someone by her side. So I'd come home, and I'd hunkered down in her house to wait for the end.

It wouldn't be long.

But the house was too quiet without her, a fact that I'd been trying to remedy by filling the silence with my own voice. The reason I'd been going through so much tea, to be honest. My throat was rough from so much use, my voice raspy. Speaking on stage for hours every night had nothing on telling her all about my life away from Justice. Admitting every secret and failure and success. Distracting us both from the inevitable, or so I hoped.

I took a sip of my tea, enjoying the warm mintiness on my throat, before I launched into more stories. "Where were we before I went to the kitchen? Oh, right. The night I nearly fell off the stage at Caesar's during a show." I sat back, almost laughing at the memory of the stage lights blinding me to the point of having no idea where I was.

Being a Vegas medium and psychic was a cool gig—one I'd worked hard at over the past decade or so. From reading tarot on the Strip to small, intimate group sessions in cafes, to selling out the theaters inside the casinos—I'd worked my way up from nothing to a level of success most people with my talent never saw. But as in any sort of show business, there were always issues. And that night, the issue had been a faulty programming note that sent the spotlight straight at my face instead of onto the floor.

I spent the better part of the afternoon sipping my tea as I regaled an unresponsive Miss with stories of accidents and mishaps, readings gone wrong and the ones that had gone too right for even me to believe. And through it all, I watched the leaves in my cup rise and settle, seeing the shapes appear that I knew would be there no matter how many times I disturbed them. The ones that spoke of loss and pain. Of death.

"I never did fit there," I whispered as the sun began to fade. My tea had long gone cold and a sharp pain had developed in my hips from sitting too long, but I didn't want to leave her side. I would never forgive myself if I let her die alone. And I already carried enough guilt.

"Vegas, I mean. I love the city, but it's never felt like home." I glanced at the homecoming picture of Bishop and me again, at my smile and the joy that radiated from the two of us. At the way his arms held me close with an obvious intimacy that came from truly knowing someone. From trusting them. I hadn't deserved his trust.

"I never got over leaving you," I said, staring at Bishop...talking to Miss. I never got over leaving either of them or the town I'd grown to love so much. The one home I'd ever had. I doubted I ever would, either. But the past was done, and there was no fixing the things I'd broken. The things I'd left behind without so much as a goodbye.

As I sat there staring at the pictures, a knock on the door echoed through the house. The sound both calmed me and ratcheted up my anxiety—company had finally come. I set down my teacup and leaned over Miss to kiss her cheek.

"That's probably the hospice nurse. I'll be right back."

My heart ached to leave her even for a minute, but I needed help. Anyone else in town would have called a Kennard. From what I understood, Alder ran the place just the way his father had before him. Supportive, succinct, and only slightly overbearing—the Kennard way.

I'd called a stranger.

A fact that ate at me the closer I came to letting this unknown person into the house. It seemed so wrong to call outsiders instead of the family who'd always been so good to the residents of Justice, but I couldn't bear to do it. So I'd dialed an unknown number instead and requested an outsider come to the house to help me get through these final hours with Miss. I'd figured anything was better than nothing in moments like these, knowing I might end up regretting that decision when this was all said and done. But the call had been made, and the person was at the door. There was no more time to waffle over my decision.

I hurried through the dark halls to the front door, trying hard to ignore how lifeless and empty the house felt. How dead already without Miss laughing and yelling through the old rooms. But it would come to life once more. I'd sell it—hopefully find a young family to move in and enjoy the odd details and funky little rooms. Maybe there'd be kids running through the halls again or a swing set outside. That would be nice. To know the life I should have built with Bishop would finally come to pass for someone else.

Someone who would hopefully cling to the gifts given to them instead of throwing them away.

And me? I'd end up alone in the desert with my thousands of fans and no real friends. No family either. Exactly as I deserved.

Chapter Three

BISHOP

There was a reason I didn't drink on work nights anymore, and that reason had caused an ache in my head that had plagued me all damn day.

"How you doing, boss?" Gage asked as he strolled into my office. The bastard had a smile on his face and looked as if he'd gotten a solid night's sleep instead of just a handful of hours. Playing off my hangover was going to take more energy than I probably had, but I'd try.

"Good, just going over some notes. You get everything squared away on the skidder?"

The skidder was a machine we used to pull the trees from where they fell to where we'd delimb, cut, and extract them. We'd gotten a call from the Hansen jobsite that the thing had stopped working, and his mechanic on site couldn't fix it. Gage had run out to Widow's Ridge to see what he could do.

"Yeah. Damn thing hung up dragging a log up the ridge because of the angle. We had to move it to a new location to ease the strain."

I'd kill for something that would ease the strain...in my head. "Good, good. What else you got for me?"

"Someone in town has requested hospice care."

Not what I had expected him to say. Ever. "Why would you know this?"

He raised a bushy eyebrow at me. "I know people."

"You've lived here like five minutes, and you *know people*? As in, better than I do?" So maybe he'd lived in Justice for five years, not minutes. Same thing around here.

Gage sat back and gave me a cocky sort of smile, barely moving the dark forest of hair on his face. "I can't help it if I like to make sure everything runs smooth around here. It's sort of why you hired me."

Technically, we'd hired him as a mechanic for our machines. True, he'd had no experience with the skidders, loaders, or delimbers we used in our operation, but that hadn't mattered. Gage could fix anything, and he'd been a loyal and trusted friend in my SEAL unit. It wouldn't have mattered if he'd never held a chainsaw or a wrench—when I left the SEALs, I brought him with me.

"Who's the patient?" I asked, thinking over all the residents of Justice who might need end-of-life care. The list was pretty damn short.

"Didn't say, but they gave me the location."

"Where?"

Gage frowned again, and my stomach turned. The feeling of something not good coming my way slammed over me and held me in its cold, hard grip as I waited for him to say the words.

"Widow's Ridge."

Every bit of air left my lungs, all my blood pooling in my shoes.

Only one residence was left up that way—the Hansen place, which meant Miss was sick.

Miss Hansen had been a staple in our town when I'd been a kid. Strong, loud, and fiery, the older woman had commanded attention whenever she'd walked in a room. Rumor had it she practiced witchcraft out on that ridge all by herself, but I'd known better. Because just as I was starting my senior year of high school, Miss Hansen had found out she had a granddaughter, and my life had changed forever.

Anabeth Monroe—born to Miss Hansen's late daughter—had spent most of her childhood in foster care, having no idea there was family out there who would have happily taken her in. By the time Miss had found out she even existed, Anabeth had been through the system enough to have walls a mile thick around her.

I'd spent two years busting those fuckers down. I'd spent another two falling in love with the red-haired woman with the vibrant smile and almost preternatural ability to know what I was thinking.

I'd spent the last almost fifteen avoiding any mention or memory of her.

"I knew Miss was sick, but I didn't think it'd gotten bad enough for all that." I stared down at the desktop, thoughts of summers in the forest and red hair sprawled out on the grass inundating my mind and making my head pound even harder. Fuck, that girl always did have the worst timing.

"Something you want to tell me about this lady? Every time her name is brought up, you get a weird look on your face. Weirder than your normal face."

I huffed a pained sort of laugh. "That's not Miss—she's amazing."

"Rumor around town is that she's a witch."

So he'd heard the same thing that had been flying around since

I'd been a kid. Funny how those whispered lies tended to stick. "Nah, at least, not like you're thinking. She's more of a spiritualist." My throat tightened and the words felt stuck as I added, "I dated her granddaughter."

"Okay." Gage sat still and calm, silent. Watching me with those dark eyes as if he could see into my soul and pluck out all my secrets. I'd never told him about Anabeth, never admitted how much she'd destroyed me. Hell, I'd never told anyone. Alder knew a little because he'd been the one to pick me up out of the gutter, but that was it. And I wasn't ready to go back down that road just yet.

"Your friend tell you who called in for assistance?" Because if Anabeth was back in town, I needed to get the fuck out before I fell right back into that old trap.

Gage waited, still watching me, but I didn't fall for that tactic. He could sit like a statue all fucking day—I wasn't opening my mouth.

After almost a minute, he must have figured that out. He picked up his phone again, pressing on the screen until he found what he wanted. "No identity of the caller. They don't have a volunteer available to head out that way for another few hours, so they were asking if one of us could run up there and make sure the family had the support they need."

I nodded, staring down at the papers on my desk. Not seeing them. "Good. Yeah. You should do that."

"You sure that's what you want?"

I shot my eyes to his as my phone rang. "Positive." And then I picked up the phone, saying my name as a greeting and getting down to the business of selling lumber.

Gage shook his head and stood, walking toward the door with Rex once again following at his heels. I stared after him as the caller babbled on about—well, fuck, I had no idea what. Didn't matter. The person on the phone had nothing on the redhead my thoughts refused to turn away from. The one who'd stolen my heart when I was still just a teenager and, sadly, never given it back. The one whose only family was probably dying up on a ridge just a few miles away.

Minutes later, after I'd ended the call, I sat and let my memories stretch a little further back than I normally allowed them to go. Let my curiosity override my need to protect myself. Let pictures of Anabeth and Miss drown me in flashbacks and feelings I'd locked up long ago. Ones that refused to let me sit there and do nothing to help the family I'd once seen as part of my own.

I needed to head up to that ridge.

I shut my laptop and grabbed my keys, unable to get Miss Hansen and her granddaughter off my mind. This was a bad plan—a horrible, no good, going to destroy everything I kept so carefully balanced sort of plan. The kind that had the potential to break me, to leave me curled up in the dirt with a bottle of something dark and dangerous. None of which could stop me.

"Gage," I snapped as soon as I hit the stairs leading to the mill floor. My mechanic leaned against the wall at the bottom with Rex at his side, both of them waiting, Gage staring up at me as if he'd known all along I'd come through that door. Fucker.

"Yeah, boss?"

"Hang back. I'll take the Hansen visit."

"Figured as much."

As I passed, he reached out and grabbed my arm. In his other hand, he held a packet of pain relievers, probably from one of the first aid kits we kept around. When I looked at him, he raised an eyebrow and waited. The bastard knew me too well.

I took the packet and tore it open. "Thanks."

"Be careful out there." He handed me a bottle of water as I swallowed the pills. "Lots to worry about on that ridge, and you've got flat-bottomed shoes on."

"You have an obsession with my shoes now?"

"I have a deep hatred for shoes that can slow you down in an emergency. You need your boots."

As if I could wear military boots on a sales call. "I'll take that under advisement."

"Which is fancy speak for *fuck off, Gage*." He smacked me on the shoulder. "Go. I'll run interference if Alder shows up looking for you."

Pain relievers in, water helping to wash them down, I gave him a serious look as we bumped fists. "You're a good man to have on a team."

"A good man who doesn't get hangovers." He grinned when I flipped him off, which was a pretty good display of exactly how our friendship worked. One of us was always trying to piss off the other. We'd probably argue about my shoes for the next week.

It was sick that I almost looked forward to that.

As soon as I got into my truck, I flipped on the wipers and glared up at the sky—the rain had finally come. The storm that would sit deep and long above us, drowning the town in water that had nowhere to go. Not a good time for Anabeth to be in Justice, if she was.

I ended up pulling into the driveway at the Hansen place way sooner than expected, having driven far too fast for the roads and the weather at hand. Fucking weak, that's what I was. Weak and worried and unsure if anyone from hospice had made it out to help. There were no cars in the driveway, and the house looked dark. Empty. For once, the liveliness of the old lady who'd lived there for as long as I could remember didn't shine through. A bad sign for sure.

Mind made up and shoulders set, I stepped out of my truck and headed for the porch.

I'd always enjoyed hanging out at Miss Hansen's house. The woman had a spirit you could practically see and a wildness to her that made for lots of laughs and fun. My family had been loud and boisterous, but not in the same way. My parents had always seemed more serious, trying hard to control the chaos that came with five energetic kids running around. Miss...well, she always had her eye on having fun. Between her gusto for life and my love for her granddaughter, I'd never regretted spending a moment in that house.

Until Anabeth had left me.

But today wasn't the day for those thoughts. Miss was likely dying, and it was my job to find out what was going on. I'd always felt a bit responsible for her. She would have been family if...

Fuck. It was definitely not the time to think about the ring still stuck in a drawer at my house or the promises that had been broken. Not at all the time.

When I reached the door, I waited. Fidgeting with my keys instead of moving to announce myself. Unsure whether to knock or haul myself back to my truck and call Gage to get his ass up here. Nervous—that was the sort of energy racing through me. Why the fuck was I nervous? I'd been a motherfucking Navy SEAL, had killed people, had walked into enemy territory and blown shit up. I didn't remember being nervous then, but faced with the possibility of a dying elderly woman and a Vegas charlatan whose lies had almost destroyed my life...

And there it was. Anabeth. The nerves were from the possibility of seeing her. Deep down, I couldn't decide if I wanted her to be inside or not, but I wouldn't know one way or the other if I didn't at least knock on the damn door.

So I knocked. And I tucked my keys into my pocket so I wouldn't fidget with them. And I waited what felt like hours for the door to open.

The kick to the gut when it did only left me more unsure than ever.

"Bishop."

One word. Anabeth Monroe said one fucking word, and the tidal wave of emotion I'd been trying to hold back for over a decade swamped me. I immediately became that same boy who'd fallen in love with her the first time he'd seen her. I'd followed her around like a goddamned puppy for years, and here I was ready to do it all again. How could I not? Everything I'd ever wanted in a woman stood before me—curves for days, big blue eyes that could practically see into my soul, long red hair that made her impossible to miss, and a heart so big she could swallow you whole with it. The hair color wasn't as bright as it had been when she was a teenager, and those curves had definitely gotten a little more dangerous over the years. But she was still my Anabeth.

Except she hadn't been mine in a long time.

I frowned, unable to stop the pull of my lips. But that was the only sign of emotion I'd give her. Back straight, head up, heart trapped under too many layers of concrete all because of the one woman staring back at me, I stared her down for a solid ten seconds before accepting the fact that it was time to actually talk to her.

"I heard Miss is sick, so I came to see how she's doing until hospice can get here."

Anabeth stared up at me, those eyes I'd wanted to wake up to every fucking morning looking watery and sad. Looking like she was a woman about to lose more than she was ready to.

"I'd ask how you heard, but I assume it's the typical Kennard family stuff—someone from the hospice center must have called the mill."

I didn't need to agree with her. The town had always been run by my family—we'd founded it, we employed it, we took care of it.

Anabeth smiled when I didn't respond, knowing the truth. An expression that didn't meet her eyes. "Please, come in. And thank you for coming. It's been a lonely couple of days."

Gut punch number two. Days? She'd been here alone with an ailing Miss for days?

"I'm surprised you didn't call us yourself," I said as I followed her inside the house. "You know we would have come to help."

The interior of Miss' house looked the same as it always had—same paint color, same wood floors and rugs, same furniture—but something felt different. Felt wrong. The house lacked the light and life that had always come right along with Miss. It felt dead, grief-stricken, in mourning already.

Anabeth took a few steps into the living room and waited, clutching a thick, heavy-looking mug in her hands. "I didn't want to be a bother to anyone."

I grunted, suddenly unsure of what to do or how to be. She didn't want me there, that much seemed obvious by her not calling. Hell, I could have sent Finn or Alder to her house if she'd told me she didn't want me around. But she'd decided to go through this alone, hiding herself away for two days before reaching out for help. Typical Anabeth—always trying to make herself invisible until she was ready to put on a show. Something else about her that hadn't really changed.

"You look good." The words came out unbidden, my brain obviously not working correctly if I was complimenting my ex.

Anabeth's plush, soft lips kicked up in a halfhearted sort of smile again. "Thanks. You do too. So much bigger than the last time..."

She didn't need to finish that sentence. Since the last time she'd seen me...when I'd chased her ass to Vegas to beg her to come back to me. Right before I'd shipped out for my first training session with the SEALs. I'd been an immature kid then, still madly in love with the woman who'd made it clear she hadn't wanted anything to do with him. One who'd made a snap decision that had altered the course of his life. Something I doubted she even knew about.

Something I had no interest in telling her. "How's Vegas?"

"It's fine." She shrugged, the curve of her collarbone drawing my eyes. "Good. Work is steady."

I locked gazes with her again, unable not to ask, "How's the guy?"

Her eyes went wide, and the cup in her hand seemed to tremble. "There is no guy."

Bullshit, but whatever. There had been a guy. I'd seen him with my own eyes, then gotten completely shit-faced on the Strip to try to drown the pain in my chest at the thought that she could have moved on so fast. There'd been others, too—tabloid stories linking her to other Vegas performers, musicians, and even an actor or two. But if she said there was no guy, I'd take comfort in that. At least I wouldn't have to see her with someone else on this trip.

"So..." I exhaled, needing to focus on the now and not the past that I couldn't fix. "Miss is sick. What are we talking about here?"

Anabeth took a deep breath, seeming to almost steel herself. "Cancer. It had metastasized by the time they found it, so she never had a real chance at treatment, though they tried. It's just...too far gone to try anymore."

Aw, fuck. I hadn't known—she'd never told me. Or maybe I'd never asked, a thought that caused guilt to weigh heavy in my gut. "I'm real sorry about that. She never let on that she was sick."

"She always did like to play her hand close to her vest."

"Just like her granddaughter."

Anabeth nodded, looking so small as she curled her shoulders. Protecting herself, holding herself together. The mug in her hand shook, the golden liquid inside splashing up enough for me to see it. Bringing back too many memories to ignore. Happy ones. The kind I'd tried to forget for over a decade.

"You still drink that fancy spearmint tea?"

Her smile grew, looking more real. "Always. Sadly, I've become addicted to a particular brand, and I'm running low already. I hadn't expected to blow through so much, but this has been harder than..."

She trailed off, staring down at her cup in silence. Probably seeing more in the leaves along the sides of the vessel than most people ever could imagine.

"Is it not something they sell over in Rock Falls?" I knew the answer—we'd had to campaign to get the little grocery store to stock any sort of loose-leaf tea back in high school. Miss and Anabeth had been the only ones who'd bought it.

Anabeth leaned a hip against the back of the couch and shook her head, tearing her eyes away from the secrets inside her cup. "Not something they sell anywhere but Texas. It's a small company—some guy who had a love of tea and heavy metal music, of all things. I've been addicted to it for over a year now."

"They ship?"

"Yeah, that's how I get it in Vegas."

"Have them send it to the mill. I'll make sure someone brings it out when it comes in."

She nodded, avoiding my gaze. "That would be nice. Thank you."

"How bad is it?" I asked, knowing she'd catch the subject change. Anabeth always had been able to follow wherever my mind went.

"It won't be long now." She took a deep breath, looking ready to cry again. "That's why I called hospice. I didn't want to leave her alone if I didn't have to."

And there I was hogging up her time and keeping her away from Miss. "I'm so sorry, Anabeth. I know how much she means to you."

She curled in on herself, holding the edges of her sweater together as if that would keep her from falling apart. But I knew her —no matter how many years away from one another, some things would never change. Anabeth only had Miss for family, and losing her would be a huge blow. One I didn't want her to have to deal with alone.

"How long are you staying?" I asked, trying hard not to care too much no matter what her answer was,

"A week or so. I'd planned to spend time with her, but..."

Her eyes welled up, her lips turning down as she seemed to fight back tears. Yeah, she'd planned to spend time with Miss, but fate wouldn't be so kind. Miss didn't have time left.

"Can I see her? I wouldn't mind saying goodbye."

Surprised blue eyes met mine. "Of course. I have her set up in her bedroom."

I followed Anabeth down the hall, focusing on the fact that I was about to have to say goodbye to someone who had meant so much to me during my youth. Trying my hardest not to notice how amazing Anabeth's ass looked in her jeans or how her hips swayed so seductively when she walked. My cock definitely noticed, though. A fact that felt all the more wrong considering the situation.

Bad timing, buddy.

But all thoughts of her curves and how much I'd like to bite them fled the second I saw Miss laid out on the bed. So small, so sickly looking...so very still.

"Jesus," I hissed, unable to hold it in. Anabeth simply nodded and waved me toward a chair next to the bed. Probably the same one she'd been sitting vigil in.

"I can leave you alone—"

I reached out and grabbed her hand before she could go, the touch electrifying even in its simplicity. Its familiarity. I hadn't touched her in fourteen years, but nothing had changed. The feel of her skin against mine still rocked my world.

Risking hell and heaven all at once, I gripped her tighter. "Stay. Please."

She stared down at our joined hands, looking so damn pained. I could practically feel the ache rolling off her. I couldn't even begin to assume it was the same ache I felt—the one that spoke of loss and need and regret. Of missed years together. She'd walked away, not me.

So I pulled my hand from hers, and I gave it instead to Miss before bowing my head in prayer. So many things to be thankful for —a strong woman like Miss to be an influence on my life, how she'd taken in Anabeth when the girl had needed her most, the happy years she'd received with the rest of us on earth. I asked for only one thing in the end—for Miss to be welcomed into whatever afterlife she believed in, for her to find her peace in death. And then I whispered a quiet amen.

"Thank you, Miss, for always watching out for us when we were younger. You were a guiding force for sure, and I benefitted from being a child in your village." I kissed the back of her hand. "May the spirits bless and keep you, and may you enjoy your next journey as much if not more than you enjoyed this one."

Anabeth rested a hand on my shoulder, branding me with her touch once more. "She would have liked that prayer."

"Good. I hope it brought her a little comfort." I patted Anabeth's hand, the one burning into my shoulder. Such torture, to have her so close again. To know there was nothing I could say to get back what we'd lost.

And there was nothing I could do to keep her from losing even more.

"C'mon," I said when a shiver wracked her body. "Let's get you another cup of tea to warm you up."

Anabeth stared at Miss for a long moment before nodding once. "Would you like a cup? I have enough to share."

"I'm never going to be a fan of that stuff, but I'll keep you company while you make one for yourself." I stood and followed her out of the room, leaving the door open just in case Miss came to and needed us. Anabeth wouldn't want to be away from her for long, that was for sure. Especially not with the way she looked back over her shoulder and into the room.

"She's okay," I said, nudging Anabeth forward. "And she'd want you to take care of yourself. Let's make the tea, then you can come back here."

She didn't look convinced, but she nodded anyway and headed toward the kitchen. "You sure you wouldn't care for a cup?"

"Not going to change my mind there."

"But if you drink it, I can read your tea leaves."

"Never going to be a fan of that either. I'd rather the future just come—I don't want to know everything beforehand."

She chuckled, her smile a little wider than before. A little more real. "At least some things never change."

Gut punch number three, and a knockout one at that. Some things didn't change, but she had. So had I. Too many years apart had caused that, too many hurts left behind. I wasn't in college anymore, wasn't young and impressionable and completely overwhelmed with all the possibilities laid out before me. She'd destroyed me then, had stolen the hope that had come with not knowing how bad things could go in life. And now? Even with my guard up and my broken heart buried beneath the sea of my own making?

She could easily do it again.

Which meant I needed to put some space between us. So as we reached the foyer, I stopped following her and instead pulled my keys from my pocket. "Actually, I should really get going. I've still got work to do tonight, and the rain's going to make the drive home a bit of a slog."

Anabeth nodded, her smile falling. "Right. Of course."

Feeling like the biggest jerk in the world, I led her to the front door, fidgeting with my keys the entire way. But when I stepped outside, I knew I couldn't leave her there like that. Not alone. I didn't even know if she had a way to reach anyone in town.

"Anabeth," I said once I stood on her front porch.

She clutched the door, not setting a toe over the threshold. Keeping us divided. "Yeah?"

"Just...here." I pulled a business card from my wallet and handed it to her as if she were some stranger, some client. Not what I'd intended, but I had no other option. "Call or text me if you need anything. Anything at all. We've had some trouble around town lately, so if you see anyone or think something feels off, let me know. I've got a team that can take care of it."

She took the card, her fingers brushing mine. A touch I felt right down to the tip of my cock. I seriously needed to get the fuck away before I did something stupid like grabbing her, kissing those soft, pink lips of hers, and begging her to take me back.

Weak. I was so utterly fucking weak for this girl.

"Vice President of Marketing and Sales. Fancy," she said, her eyes locked on the card and her face carefully blank. Apparently not as affected as I was. Something to remember. "Thank you for this. I appreciate it."

Done. Over. Nothing more to say. Without another word, I turned and walked away. Needing air. Needing a minute to collect myself. To remember why I had to leave her there. Why it was so stupid to come back. By the time I reached my truck, Anabeth had disappeared into the house and closed the door. Gone again. Always fucking gone, that girl. Always would be too, so there was no reason to think this time might be different.

Time had changed some things, but not that fact. Anabeth wouldn't stay, and I had no interest in letting her destroy me when she left again.

Chapter Four

BISHOP

I fell asleep that night to thoughts of Anabeth and the sound of rain. Woke up to them both, too. The rain won out as the most worrisome. Steady, solid, and heavy, the water poured from the sky. It continued as I got ready for the day, as I did my best not to think about Anabeth and Miss, and as I slugged back a second cup of coffee. I needed to get to work, to make sure the mill was ready for the storm that would likely shut us down for a few days. That would definitely give me something to focus on besides my past.

The drive in sucked, the roads already slick and the run-off areas already filling. We were in for a walloping with this storm, that was for sure. And if the faces of the men working the mill floor were any indication, they all knew it.

We needed to prepare. There was a creek out behind the mill that would likely breach its banks. As usual, Alder seemed to be one step ahead of me.

"Sand will be here in twenty," he yelled as he walked in through the rear door of the mill. "We're going to need to bolster the back doors and the north wall of the mill to keep the water out. Once we're done, we'll be filling bags for town. This is our day, gentlemen. No lumber, no harvest, no orders going out. We're bagging sand."

I was still setting up the bags for filling, waiting on the sand delivery, when I received a text message from an unknown number. I assumed it would be work-related, but something about the time, about the darkness of the day, and maybe even some sort of intuition had me swiping to check.

It wasn't about work.

Miss died this morning.

Anabeth. The world stopped, the pain those words caused amplified by the knowledge that she'd likely been alone up there when her grandmother passed. Had been forced to deal with such a loss without a shoulder to lean on or a hand to hold. Anabeth was a strong woman—independent and intelligent and an army of one for sure—but she was still just a girl losing her last family member. All by herself.

Guilt had never felt so cold.

"Something wrong?"

I looked up from my phone, meeting Alder's concerned gaze. Hell, every one of the mill guys was looking at me. I could only imagine what they'd seen on my face to make them stop like that.

"Miss Hansen died this morning."

The men around us seemed to take a collective breath. Miss Hansen had been well-known and liked in town for decades. She was a force in my own life but also for just about every man in that room.

Alder sighed, a tic in his jaw the only sign that this news hit him at all. I didn't need to tell him who the message was from for him to know. "You should go."

I looked back at my phone. No request for help, no sign that she needed me in the least. Still, I had to make sure.

What can I do?

The bubbles indicating an incoming reply appeared almost instantly. I couldn't look away from the screen, not sure whether I wanted to see her ask for help for once in her life or not. Not sure which response would make me feel less impotent when it came to her.

Her answer didn't take long.

Thanks, but I'm okay right now. The Molnar's Funeral Home people are here to take her to Rock Falls. Once they're done, I'm heading to their offices to make her final arrangements and will let you know the details once I get back.

No help needed.

"Doesn't appear that she needs me." As if she ever had.

"She'll have to call the funeral home," Alder said. "Make arrangements for a service."

"She says she's heading there now."

"You should go with her."

I started to shake my head no, but Alder stopped me with a look.

"I had to make every decision when Dad died. Sitting in old man Molnar's office and picking out the coffin, the ceremony, the suit for his body...it was the loneliest two hours of my life." Alder laid a hand on my shoulder, his eyes holding mine. His face too damn serious. "I understand you have history with her, stuff that I don't even know, but she's alone out there and this is her only family. She needs someone right now, which is our job as caretakers of this town and its residents."

But life with Anabeth had never been that simple. "And what if that someone isn't me?"

"What if it is?"

I slipped my hand into my pocket, fiddling with the keys there.

Sandbags and water levels and constant rain bombarded my thoughts, but none of that was enough to cover the image of blue eyes and red hair that haunted me. Of her crumpled and crying over the body of her grandmother. Of her in pain.

Decision made. "I'll be back later to help with the sandbags."

"Yeah, yeah. You say that now." Alder waved me off, turning back to get to work before hollering, "Be careful out there."

I wasn't sure if he meant to be careful in the rain, careful that I didn't have a run-in with the Soul Suckers, or careful with my heart around Anabeth. Any of the three could be deadly, really.

Too many minutes later, I turned onto the sloppy, muddy road that led to the Hansen property. The creek it crossed wouldn't take much more to top its banks just like down by the mill, and the road would likely be blocked. If the earthen dam higher up the mountain—the one that controlled the flow from the melting snowcaps all summer—failed, the road would likely be completely washed away. Anabeth would be stuck up in that house all alone, with no way to come into town. No way to get help if she needed it.

That would need to be dealt with, and soon.

My truck slid as I pulled into her driveway, practically hydroplaning on the standing water. The ground was already sodden, the limits of the area reached. A flood was definitely coming, one that we could only hope wouldn't wreak too much havoc. I had enough of that to deal with.

I hurried to the porch and knocked on the door, hoping Anabeth hadn't left yet. Not wanting to be too late...again. She opened the door a few seconds later, her chin up and her makeup on but her face pink and streaked with tears. Looking so fucking beautiful and fierce in her grief.

Putting on a show.

"Bishop," she whispered, reminding me of the day before when

I'd shown up the same way—uninvited, possibly unwanted, but needing to be there.

"Thought you could use a friend today."

And for possibly only the second time since I'd met her, that rock-hard facade broke. Her shoulders slumped, her body curling in on itself as she surrendered to her grief. Every inch of her softened, and tears fell down her pale, freckled cheeks unabashed. Broke wasn't a strong enough word. She crumbled right in front of me.

There was nothing to do but reach for her, grab her, and pull her into my arms. The way I used to when I knew she needed affection but was too damn scared to ask for it. The way I did the night before I left for college, holding her close and promising her that we would always be us. The way I did that last spring break week, when I'd made love to that girl knowing I'd be asking her to marry me in just a few short months.

The way I'd been wanting to do again for fourteen long fucking years.

Anabeth clung to my arms, shaking, sobbing silently against me. There was no stopping the feeling of rightness that pelted me with her against my chest. No way to protect myself from falling that much deeper into an attraction I knew would drown me.

My heart still wanted her, possibly more than ever before.

And I was going to hate myself when she broke it again.

***

ANABETH

The ride back from the funeral home seemed to take forever. Or maybe I was too tired from all the activity that morning and desperate to take to my bed. My grandma's death hadn't hit me yet, not really, but I knew it would. I'd cracked a little when Bishop had shown up at my door, but the dam holding back my emotions hadn't fully broken. It would. And soon.

He needed to drive faster.

"You okay?"

I turned away from the window, shrugging. I couldn't look at him, not fully, not without breaking all that much sooner. Instead, I focused on his hands as they gripped the steering wheel. On those long, thick fingers that could be so gentle. That had held my hand and stroked my arm as I'd sat in the office at the funeral home going over wood tones for the urn her ashes would be put into and if I wanted flowers, music, and a video presentation with pictures of my grandmother alive scrolling past. As I'd decided all the things that would cement the fact that the one person who'd ever shown me a drop of true care and love was gone.

Well, one person other than the man currently driving me home.

"As much as I can be." I watched as his fingers tightened, as the muscles in his wrists seemed to flex. I could practically feel the tension radiating off of him—he didn't like my answer. I almost smiled at that. He always had wanted me to open up more. And perhaps that wasn't such a bad idea. "Thanks for coming with me. I really do appreciate it."

His grip loosened. "I know how much Miss meant to you."

She had. She really had. That woman hadn't even known I'd existed when my mother—her only daughter—had died. The two hadn't spoken in years from what she'd told me, and she'd been shocked to discover the daughter she'd raised and lost had had a daughter of her own. But by that time, I'd already been in and out of foster homes for most of my life. Being the child of an addict wasn't easy or safe. Every time my mother got busted for possession or soliciting, I'd been taken away and sent to live with strangers again.

Some were nice, some were...not so nice. None of them truly seemed to care about me.

But then Miss had shown up at my caseworker's office with a lawyer by her side. She'd actually *asked* me if I wanted to come stay with her, had taken the time to introduce herself and tell me about what life with her as my guardian would be like.

I'd jumped at the chance.

So Miss had taken me home with her, and I'd moved in to her little farmhouse on the ridge surrounded by a forest so deep and old, it made me feel wonderfully invisible. She'd taught me about the gifts she'd been born with, the ones that showed her glimpses of the future, the ones that settled the tea leaves just so or influenced her to pull a particular card from the tarot deck. Miss taught me to stand up for myself, to use my charm to my advantage, to brew the perfect cup of tea, and to understand that not all in the world was as it appeared.

She'd taught me to be me, and now she was gone.

Seriously, Bishop needed to drive faster before the dam holding my heart together broke and I flooded his truck with my tears.

"Is this rain ever going to let up?" I asked, trying hard to focus on something other than the pain building inside of me.

"I sure do hope so, but it's a stalled front. We're in for a world of hurt if it doesn't move along soon."

"You think we might have a flood?"

"I think there are a lot of old earthen dams up in these hills that have seen too much drought lately. I don't trust them to hold up. Plus, the ground's too hard and dry to absorb much of this. That's why there's standing water already on your driveway—it has nowhere to go."

He would know—he'd spent more time exploring the mountainside and learning about this area than any of the other

Kennard boys. "Well, I hope it stops soon. I'd like to head into town and see what's changed. Maybe hike a bit up in the hills."

Bishop stayed silent for a long minute, the only sound the rumble of the engine and the thump of the wiper blades as they slid back and forth over the windshield.

"That's a bad idea," he finally said. My eyes darted to his face of their own volition, my head cocking as I took in the heavy frown he wore.

"Why do you say that?"

"We've had trouble recently."

I nearly rolled my eyes. "I know my way around these woods. Besides, I can take care of myself."

"Or the guys causing trouble can show up and take care of you themselves."

"Well, that's quite the positive take on something so simple."

"That's reality, sweetheart."

His words caused the doors inside of me to slam closed, flooding my mind with anger and frustration. I hated it when men called me sweetheart in that tone. The one that practically mocked me, as if I had no clue what I was talking about. I worked in Vegas—men with more money than morals, mob bosses, and shady characters were a staple in my world. I wasn't ignorant of how badly things could go, but apparently Bishop thought I was.

If Miss hadn't raised me to be kind when someone took the time to help me, I'd have called him an asshole.

Instead, I kept my mouth shut the rest of the way back to the farmhouse, my leg shaking and my arms crossed. Stiff. Unyielding. Maybe I wouldn't cry once I got inside—maybe I'd throw some breakables to use up the raging frustration flowing through me.

Maybe I'd throw things at Bishop.

But frustration and irritation reminded me of other things, of times when Bishop had pushed me just like he was now, and I'd lashed out at him. We'd fight, me flying off the handle and him staying irritatingly calm until I'd crack. Until I'd go to slap his hand away or push him back when he tried to corner me, and I'd grab him instead. Hold him close. Until the emotions flooding me would take a turn from anger to lust, and I'd kiss that annoying smirk right off his handsome face.

I needed to get away from him before I did something utterly stupid. Because I would. I wanted to. Wanted to feel a connection to someone so badly.

The second he came to a stop in my driveway, I pushed open the door and stepped out into the storm, escaping. "Thanks for the ride."

Bishop wouldn't let me go, though. Of course not. He jumped down on his side, hurrying around the front of the truck after me. "Anabeth, wait. Listen to me."

He grabbed my arm, stopping me in my tracks. I slipped at the abruptness of it, but Bishop would never let me fall. Even soaking wet, the man had the strength to hold me up. His touch went from gentle and safe to harder and more dangerous, though. One hand on my arm, the other sliding down to my hip. Holding me in place with his fingers brushing against my ass. Tugging me against his chest to keep me on my feet. Bringing us together from shoulders to knees.

Touching. So much touching.

The rain had already soaked us both to the bone, but it didn't matter. I couldn't look away from him, couldn't care that I was wet and cold. I shivered, the damp air stealing all my body heat. Or maybe that wasn't just the weather, because Bishop had his hands on me. And he wasn't letting go. Instead, he stared down at me with heat and fire in his eyes, with his want so obvious. So wild. So close. His face, his lips, those steel-gray eyes I had always loved so much were all so very close to me. Right up against me.

And just like I remembered, he smelled of spearmint.

The dam inside of me finally burst, but it wasn't sadness that came rushing over me. I lunged forward, clinging to his shoulders as I pressed my lips to his. As I stole a kiss from him. Bishop didn't hesitate to respond—didn't freeze or balk or recoil. No, the man dove right in with me, picking me up off the ground and wrapping my legs around his waist as his tongue invaded my mouth. As he took over my simple act and turned it into something more, something so hot and wet, so strong. Into a kiss that refused to be tamed.

There was nothing gentle or kind about the act, nothing sweet. Bishop gripped me as if afraid I'd pull away, his fingers digging deep into my flesh. Demanding I stay. His tongue slicked against mine like it belonged there, his lips refusing to release me. This was more than a kiss, it was a take-over—hostile and rough. Almost painful in its intensity. Almost perfect in its force.

A kiss fourteen years in the making.

Unable to stop, unable to hold still, I rolled my hips against his, pressing against the hard ridge between us. Loving the little grunt he gave and wanting so much more from him. But the rain never let up, and the cold finally got to me. As lightning flashed from across the valley, I trembled, breaking the kiss and pressing my forehead against his as I caught my breath. As I fought to control the way my heart wanted to leap out of my chest.

"Fuck, Anabeth," Bishop said, panting as he let my legs slide back to the ground. As he held me tight and kept his big body against mine. "What are we doing?"

That question pulled me up fast. What *were* we doing? Or rather, what was I doing... Other than making even more mistakes. I couldn't hurt him again. I couldn't take him down that same path only to walk away. Or have him leave me behind.

"I'm sorry." I pulled out of his hold, curling in on myself. "I shouldn't have done that."

Bishop's face hardened and he looked away, his anger rolling off him in waves. "Shouldn't have, but you did."

I did. And I wanted to do it again, which made me whisper another, "I'm sorry."

"You said that." He pinned me with a hard glare, those steely gray eyes burning. "What do you want, Anabeth? What do I need to do here?"

Kiss me again. Tell me it'll be okay. Make me feel something other than pain and loss.

All impossible things. So I lied. "Nothing. I want nothing."

"Nothing. From me."

The hurt in his voice killed me, but I held my tongue. Of course I wanted things from Bishop Kennard. I wanted more of his kisses, to see him look at me with love and affection, to have his warm body wrapped around mine at night. I wanted to share stories of our days over dinner and wake up to his smiling face. I wanted everything— but I didn't deserve a single bit of it. I didn't deserve him.

When I didn't speak again, he grunted a frustrated sort of noise, his lips twisting into a frown. "Fine. I'll give you your *nothing*, Anabeth."

He spun on his heel and stormed off, heading for his truck. Leaving me behind just as I'd left him. And as I stood there in the rain, as the cold and the loss and the grief pulled me under the foamy waves, I knew the pain and heartbreak building inside of me was exactly what I deserved for lying to him. Again.

Chapter Five

ANABETH

Do not think about kissing Bishop or the reversed nine of wands card you pulled this morning. Think about...

"It will never stop raining," I said to no one, frowning out the windshield at the constant sheet of water falling from the sky. One of the only things I didn't miss about living along the Rocky Mountain Front was the rainy season. Sure, it rained in Vegas—rained hard enough to flood the streets sometimes—but not like in Justice. In Vegas, the rain came and went faster than dollar bills in a slot machine. In Justice, the rain clouds rolled in heavy and dark, blocking the top of the mountains as they settled in for days upon days of nothing but cold, wet skies. It often felt as if you'd never see the sun again, that the rain clouds would stay up against that mountain range and the world would simply fade to black along with them.

Or perhaps my mind wasn't in the right place to be dealing with so much darkness while preparing for a funeral. I'd pulled some bad

47

cards that morning, including my least favorite—the nine of wands reversed. It indicated hesitancy and being on edge in my life, things I definitely felt. Things I needed to confront and address if I was to move forward, but I couldn't focus on that. Instead, my mind kept rolling through memories of the night before. Of a kiss that never should have happened and a fight afterward. Of a certain local with strong lips and even stronger hands.

Quit thinking about Bishop.

I drove through Justice, heading back from Rock Falls with a trunk full of grocery bags. I hadn't been able to do any sort of shopping with Miss sick, the days leading up to her death too stressful to try. But life always moved on, which meant I needed supplies. And distractions.

The old house had been too quiet when I'd woken up that morning. Too dark and empty. There was a lot to do there—clean out the closets and cubbies, rearrange the furniture so I could put it up for sale, prepare to say goodbye and grieve every single aspect of my former life forever—but all that could wait for half a day. I needed a couple of hours out of the house, away from the loneliness and the sadness that had infested it. At least, that's what I'd told myself when I'd gone running out the front door that morning as if chased by a ghost.

As I turned onto Main Street, I spotted a new sign along the strip of mostly empty buildings. The Baker's Cottage. Catchy in a homey sort of way, and a complete surprise. A restaurant actually in town? A sign in the window said "Now Open," and another said "Homemade Soup Daily." A hot, hearty bowl of soup sounded like the perfect thing to combat the dreariness of the day, and I wasn't ready to face the afternoon alone in that empty house, so I pulled into a parking spot.

A bell chimed quietly overhead when I walked into The Baker's Cottage, adding to the quaintness of the warm, ski-lodge style interior. Soft, muted grays made the perfect backdrop for the wood trim around the walls and ceilings, and the rocks stacked to form the bar fit right into the space. Someone knew the area well. The locals should have been flocking there, but the restaurant sat empty instead. Odd, even for a late morning in Justice. And a perfect issue to focus on so I could stop thinking about...other things.

"Hi there." A pixie-like young woman with her blond hair pulled up in a sleek ponytail appeared from the back. "Welcome to The Baker's Cottage. Can I get you some coffee?"

I slid onto a stool at the bar and reached for a menu. "No, thanks. I'm more of a tea girl."

"You and the owner must be kindred souls." She pulled a wooden box from under the counter. "We've got options from some of the best tea blenders around the country. What's your preference? Black, green, oolong?"

"Green. I usually drink a spearmint tea."

"Then I know just the one." She turned to add water to the electric kettle behind her, humming softly to herself. I'd learned early to trust my instincts about people, and that had paid off well for me in Vegas. I might not truly see someone's future like Miss had been able to, but I could play the part of the seer. I could prod enough to get a reaction, to make the mark show a sign of positive or negative response, and build from there. My skills lay in reading tarot cards, but even that required an understanding of people to get a true and honest read on them.

This girl? Happiness practically radiated off of her, and I found myself wondering if she was newly married or pregnant. Maybe both. I reached into my bag and pulled out my tarot deck, wanting to read her cards. Wanting to know more about her. I shuffled the deck quickly, fingering the edges before flipping one, then two, then three, all while focusing on the blonde across the bar. Me pulling the cards wouldn't give me an exact read on her, but it'd be a start.

Something unobtrusive and quiet I could do to learn more. And if she saw and asked me to give her an actual read? All the better.

The first card came up as the knight of cups, indicating romance and a knight in shining armor in her life. If she didn't have a partner, and one who protected her at all costs, I'd be surprised. The second showed me the fool—innocence and new beginnings. The third brought a frown to my face—a reversed wheel of fortune card indicating bad luck and external forces against her. That didn't fit, but I couldn't tell if the card was meant for her or for me, or if it was just a bad pull.

"Justice is a small town," the waitress said, smiling politely as she grabbed a tea bag from the box before me. "I don't think I've seen you around. Passing through?"

I slipped the wheel of fortune card back into the deck. She didn't need to know about that one. Sometimes being a good performer meant hiding the bad things from those around you, especially when they hadn't asked to know about them.

"Sort of. Lived here for a while back in high school, then headed off to Vegas. My grandmother's from here, though. Or she was." I had to find a better explanation when she gave me a confused look. "She just passed. Sorry—I'm not really used to thinking of her as gone yet."

"I'm so sorry for your loss." She cocked her head, looking at me in a new light then glancing down to the cards on the bar in front of me. "Are you Miss Hansen's granddaughter? The one who tells people their futures?"

"Sure am." I smiled and offered my hand. "I'm Anabeth Monroe. And you are?"

"No way." A brunette practically slid through the door to the kitchen, her eyes wide and her smile wider. "Anabeth Monroe. I never thought I'd see that red hair in person again."

It took me less than three seconds to pull up the memories of that wide smile and those pretty hazel eyes. Katie Baker—she'd been a few years behind me in school, but I remembered her. She'd spent most of her time with the youngest Kennard sibling, a girl named Lainie. Short and rail thin back in those days, Katie had grown into a curvy woman with a welcoming smile and a body that would knock a grown man on his ass. I would have bet she was super popular with the men at the mill.

"Katie." I stood and hugged the shorter girl. "Is this your place? I didn't even know you were still in town."

"I wasn't, but I am now. Just came back, actually." She moved behind the bar, joining the blonde. "I moved to Denver for a bit to go to culinary school and try to be a chef in the city, but ended up missing home too much. So I'm here, and I've just opened this place. With a little help from the Kennards, of course."

Of course. Nothing happened in this town without them. "Well, the restaurant looks amazing, and the soup choices sound delicious."

"Thanks. I'm pretty proud of what I've done so far." Her eyes went wide, her mouth falling open as she reached for me. "I'm also an asshole. Here I am talking about opening a restaurant, and you're dealing with grief. I heard Miss passed away. I'm so sorry. Is there anything I can do?"

That was something I desperately missed about small-town life —the family vibe. The way neighbors looked out for one another. The gossip flew pretty fast, but so did the offers of help when you needed it.

Didn't mean I could accept it, though. "Thank you, but I'm fine. Everything is handled, and now I just have to wait for the actual funeral."

"It's Saturday, right?"

Two days until I had to say goodbye to Miss forever. "Yeah, at Molnar's in Rock Falls."

"Well, you can count on me being there." Katie gave me a supportive sort of smile and covered my hand with hers. "What else can I do? Are you hungry? Of course you are—you're in a restaurant. What can I get you?"

"I saw your sign in the window and thought a warm bowl of soup sounded like perfection on such a dreary day. I was about to try to pick when you came in."

Katie slid the menu back in front of me. "Soup is a good choice. Besides what's on the menu here, I've got a steak stew that's been simmering since four this morning. It's probably the best stew I make, if you're up for more of a hearty meal."

"That sounds perfect."

"I'll get it," the blonde said, moving toward the kitchen. Katie stopped her before she could pass, though.

"Anabeth, have you met Shye yet?"

I smiled and offered my hand again. "I was just introducing myself when you came out. Hi, I'm Anabeth Monroe."

"Shye Anderson," she said, shaking my hand. "It's nice to meet you."

"Shye's somewhat new in town," Katie said. "Though she's already locked down Alder Kennard."

Locked down...I hadn't been wrong about her. "Alder's married? I had no idea."

Shye rolled her eyes. "We're not married, though he'd drag me down to the courthouse right this second if I let him."

She joked, but the blush on her cheeks and the light in her eyes didn't lie—the woman was in love. In deep.

My smile got a little harder to hold on to.

"Well, congratulations. The Kennards are good people, and if these cards are right—and they're always right"—I pasted on my stage grin and winked her way—"you've got a happy future with hope and possibility coming your way. You should definitely let him drag you wherever he wants to take you."

"All in good time," Shye said, still grinning, still practically glowing with a happiness she seemed to be trying to rein in. "I'm really sorry to hear about Miss, though. She was always kind to me when I lived up on the ridge."

"Thank you. I'm glad you got to know her before she passed."

Katie bumped shoulders with the woman. "All right, Mrs. Kennard. How about you go grab her a bowl of stew before your bodyguard shows up?"

Shye frowned, then disappeared into the back as Katie poured my steeped tea.

"Bodyguard?"

Katie hummed. "You'll see. So tell me—how's Vegas?"

I shrugged, ambivalent about my adopted home, ripping the corner of my paper napkin to keep my hands busy so I didn't reach for my cards again. "Fine. Good. My career is going well, and I've got a nice place far enough off the Strip to not have to deal with tourists very often. What more could I ask for?"

More kisses from Bishop.

As if reading my mind, Katie asked, "Got a man out there?"

"No. No man." To be truthful, I hadn't had a boyfriend since Bishop. I'd dated. I'd even tried for a commitment at one point, but no dice. Every time someone got too close, I ran. Romance didn't seem to be in the cards for me no matter what the local gossip hounds liked to think. They stirred up trouble whenever they saw me even talking to another man, which did nothing but irritate me.

Kissing Bishop didn't irritate you... The memory of the day before, of throwing myself at Bishop and how he'd kissed me, screamed through my mind. It had been a great kiss—intense and soul-shattering—but that was all it could be. A single kiss. I'd told him I wanted nothing from him, and if the silence of my cell phone was any indication, he was following my directive. Which was for the best. Or so I told myself.

Shye returned with the stew and a roll before disappearing into the back again, leaving Katie and me in the otherwise empty dining room. The other woman busied herself behind the bar as I brought a spoonful of stew to my mouth. An explosion of flavors erupted, the warmth pushing aside the constant chill that had settled upon me.

"Oh my god," I said as soon as I lifted another spoonful up to blow on it. "This is amazing."

"Thanks. It was my grandma's recipe, but I changed a few things around. Classic with a twist, you know?" Katie's grin dropped into a concerned frown as she looked past me. "Now if I could just get about a hundred more customers to be willing to give me a shot, everything would be just peachy."

"I noticed you were a bit slow. I'd have figured the guys at the mill would be all over a place like this."

"I'm sure they'll come around once things settle back down." She shrugged when I didn't respond. "They've had some trouble with the Soul Suckers lately."

That was something you didn't hear every day. "Soul Suckers... The mill's had problems with demons?"

"No, not demons. The motorcycle gang," Shye said, appearing from the back just as the bell over the door dinged for a new customer. A man I didn't recognize—long hair, beard, flat, dark eyes, and enough muscle to be a threat even if he smiled your way. Which he was not. Living in Vegas and doing the job I did—reading the people in a crowd and figuring how to push their buttons—I knew when bad entered a room, and that man was bad.

Tiny Shye simply huffed, looking like a kitten about to use its claws. "My chaperone is here."

Katie shook her head, watching the bearded one with something like interest. Something she definitely seemed to be trying to hide. "Alder worries about you. We should all be so lucky as to have a man watching out for us."

"I know. I just wish things didn't have to be so complicated." Shye shot me a smile tinged with frustration. "It was nice meeting you, Anabeth."

"You as well," I said as I watched the woman walk out with the bear of a man who...hadn't said a single word.

"So that's the bodyguard."

"Yup." Katie waited until I had a spoonful of stew in my mouth to say, "They burned her trailer."

I choked and sputtered, grabbing my napkin to cover my mouth as I gasped, "They what?"

"The Soul Suckers Motorcycle Club. They set her trailer on fire and burned it to the ground."

I couldn't believe that, but Katie certainly didn't look as if she were joking. "Really?"

Katie nodded. "You remember Camden and Leah?"

A picture formed in my mind, one of friends from school. A couple I'd spent enough time around to remember well. "Yeah. Are they still together?"

"They were. The Soul Suckers burned his house too. Leah died in the fire."

My stomach dropped. I remembered them both from high school—they'd hung out a lot at the Kennard house because of Camden's friendship with the twins. Leah had always been kind and polite, a little quiet but a woman with a huge smile for the people she cared about.

And they'd murdered her.

That had to be what Bishop had meant the day before when he'd said there'd been trouble. He hadn't wanted me alone and in the woods, not because he was being an overbearing ass, but because there was real danger lurking out there.

I was an idiot. "When did all this happen?"

"Started a few weeks ago. Alder sort of went a little heavy-handed after the fires. He's had the town on lockdown to keep everyone as safe as he can. I had to fight to stay open, though I'm not sure it's worth the hours I put in, you know? When the mill guys come in, they come in groups. The rest of the time, nothing."

"Oh, Katie. I'm sorry. This place is great—I know it'd do well if all this weren't going on."

"Me too. And it's why I moved back—to get a chance to do something in town. I spent my teenage years running away from here every chance I could get because there was nothing, you know? And then I really did run—my mom and I moved to Denver, so I finished school there. But after she died, I wanted to set up shop and serve the community where I'd grown up, just like the Bell family does over at Bell's Hardware. I wanted to fill an opening in town, but I might not make it if customers don't show up." She tossed a towel on the counter, sighing and shaking her head. "If I could maybe get everyone in town here at once—"

"You should have a grand opening party." The words fell from my lips without thought, but they felt right. Too many years working the Strip and hoping to get my name recognized had left me with a strong intuition about what would attract a crowd. Alder Kennard wanted people in groups to keep them safe? We could give him one big group. "Something fun and super family friendly. Like when the mill used to put on the fall festival. Do they still do that?"

Katie shrugged, though I could see the excitement brimming in her eyes. "I'm not sure. I just moved back this spring, but with the Soul Suckers issue, I don't know if they will this year."

"You should push for that, see if the Kennards will allow a fall festival right here at The Baker's Cottage to give your restaurant a boost. I'll do what I can to help if I'm still in town."

She grabbed my hand, her big eyes locked on mine. "Would you do a show here? Like, a walking tarot card reading or something? I've seen you on YouTube—you're amazing, and I bet everyone in town would come to see you perform."

Humility forced me to shrug as if her words didn't bring me joy. I'd worked hard to get to where I was—had given up everything so I could focus on a career I had never even dreamed possible. I was proud of how far I'd come, even if the thrill of being in front of a crowd had faded over the years.

Even if I'd give it all up in a second to get back what I'd lost.

Which was something I wouldn't be admitting out loud. "I'd be happy to perform here if you want me to. I only have about a week in town, though."

"I want, I want—and I can totally work with your schedule. Oh, this will be wonderful!" Katie bounced on the balls of her feet, clapping her hands as she babbled on about themes and plans and what dishes she could make. I sat and finished my stew, basking in the joy she radiated. After so many days of dreariness and pain, it was a nice change.

One that collapsed into a cold, hard ball of regret when the bell over the door dinged again.

Finn Kennard. The man who'd made a decision as a teenager that had sent my life skittering sideways, destroying so much. Taking everything away from me, more than even he knew. My former best friend stood there, looking so much older than the last time I'd seen him. More haggard in some ways. Harder. And damn, did I want to hug him and punch him in the face at the same time.

"I heard you were in town." He approached me warily, slowly, each step precise. I turned on my stool and did my best to smile. I hadn't seen him since right after that last day we'd spent in the woods of the east ridge. He'd come to apologize for what had happened, but I'd slammed the door in his face. And then I'd left town.

He'd written me countless letters while he was in prison, all full of apologies and regret. All obviously him trying to work his twelve steps to recovery. I'd torn up each one and flushed the pieces down the drain. Too flooded with guilt and pain and rage to acknowledge them. Until the last one—the letter he'd written when he'd gotten out. The one that said he'd never forgive himself for what he'd done. The one that said he wished he could go back in time so he could relive that day a different way. I wished for the same thing, though for reasons he wasn't even aware of. Things I'd hidden. But all the wishing in the world wouldn't bring back what I'd lost. Time couldn't be erased, and my decisions had been my own, no matter how much I still wanted to blame someone for the results of them.

I'd written back a simple, handwritten card that said, "I can forgive you for your actions, but I'll never forgive myself."

Since I'd promised forgiveness, I figured I'd at least have to try. Starting immediately.

"You're looking good, young man."

His grin exploded across his face, making him appear ten years younger. "Not as good as you, hot stuff."

"Aw, there goes that Kennard charm, working me over again."

His gait stuttered, and his smile dropped just a little. An icy chill spread through my chest, the pain it brought nearly stealing my breath. That Kennard charm had worked me over before, too. Bishop's. But it wasn't the time for thoughts like that, especially with Katie looking on.

"Seriously. How are you, Finn?" He looked clean and sober to me; I certainly hoped he was.

"I'm okay," he said, rolling his eyes when I cocked my head.

"Promise. I'm doing fine. How are you handling everything? I'm so damn sorry to hear about Miss."

Hearing her name, being reminded of my loss, was like an icicle to the heart—cold and painful. "I'm doing okay, considering."

"Yeah, it's not easy. The death of my dad left me pretty wrecked for almost a year, so I get it. Let me know if you need anything, okay?"

I wouldn't need anything from him, but I smiled anyway. "Of course. Thanks."

He looked beyond me, nodding. "Hey, Katie. Can I get a quart of the cream of chicken and a piece of whatever pie you've got? To go."

"Sure thing, Finn. Cream of chicken and lemon meringue, coming up." She headed for the back, leaving us alone together for the first time in too many years to count. I couldn't hold his gaze, couldn't look in that face that had brought me so much happiness and pain. Couldn't—

"You should tell him."

The world stopped, stuttered. Came back to life again with me as a passenger, spinning too fast to get my bearings. To see straight. To do anything but whisper, "It's too late for that."

"He's my brother. I know him—it's never too late when it comes to you."

Damn it, I wasn't ready for that conversation. Wasn't ready to even think of such things. Thankfully, I didn't need to. Katie had perfect timing, walking through the door holding a brown paper bag with handles before I needed to reply.

"Here you go, Finn."

He stepped away, reaching for the bag. "You've got my card on file?"

"Yeah. Though, seriously—learn to carry a wallet."

He met my eyes again, serious. So damn haunted. "My memory's not as good as it used to be."

Too bad mine was, which ruined what little appetite I had.

"Katie, this was excellent." I reached for my purse, but Finn shook his head.

"Add her lunch to mine."

"You don't have to do that."

"It's the least I can do." He grabbed his bag from Katie and headed toward the door, giving me room. Not letting me go just yet, though. "Let me walk you to your car."

I slid off the stool and smiled at the woman behind the bar, figuring she'd be gossiping about my interaction with the younger Kennard twin if she still had friends in town. "It was good to see you again, Katie. Let me know if there's anything you need my help with for the grand opening party."

"I definitely will but not until after the funeral. You take your time to grieve."

"I appreciate that."

"Of course. And thanks for coming in."

Finn led me outside, holding the door like a gentleman. "I'm real sorry about Miss. Her death will leave a hole in this town for sure."

"Thanks. It's so different up on that ridge without her, you know? Almost...eerie."

He pulled me to a stop, his hold gentle. Not demanding in any way. "The ridge isn't as safe as it once was. Can I... Will you give me your number so I can reach you if anything goes down?"

Hesitancy, paranoia, being on edge and defensive... The reversed nine of wands card, making itself known. It wasn't the time to make hasty judgments. Besides, this was Finn. Former best friend. Former confidant. And before the drugs took hold of him, one of the few people I actually trusted. We didn't have to be friends, but having someone to reach out to other than Bishop was probably a good idea. "Sure. Of course."

He handed me his phone, and I quickly typed in my contact information before giving it back to him. He sent me a text right away with a fish emoji as the message. Something that made me smile again.

"Smartass."

"Always." He opened my car door for me, hanging on to the top of it as I slid into my seat. "Call me if you need anything. Anytime— doesn't matter. I'll be available. And be careful up there."

"I will." I buckled my belt, waving one last time as he shut my door before walking toward an old, deep blue pickup truck. I could only describe seeing him as bittersweet—I was thrilled he seemed healthy, so glad he looked clean and sober. But his face still caused an ache within me, his presence making my anxiety stand up and scream. I'd lost everything because of one mistake, and Finn sat at the heart of it. I'd lost my family, my future, and my place in this town. I'd lost Bishop, too—quite likely the only man I would ever love.

And there was no way I could ever get that back.

Not after what I did.

Not after what I had destroyed with Finn's help.

Chapter Six

BISHOP

Twenty hours of silence. All of Wednesday night and Thursday without a single text or call. That's what I got after leaving Anabeth behind on that mountain. Almost a full day of not hearing from her. My phone stayed in my hand for those long hours, my mind unable to stop focusing on that kiss, on the feel of her body wrapped around mine once more, the taste of her on my lips.

But she'd shut down on me, told me she wanted nothing from me. So I'd given her nothing.

I'd sped down the mountain road far too fast to be safe, pissed and hurt and feeling so fucking stupid. I'd seen that wall go up behind her eyes, had felt how she'd pulled away from me both physically and emotionally. She'd locked herself down tight, just like she used to when we were younger. Back then, I'd have stayed on that porch begging her to come out and talk to me until I wore her down or Miss made me leave.

I wasn't a teenager anymore.

So I'd driven away, fuming as I'd pushed my truck to the limit down the highway. I'd refused to reach out to her in any way until she reached first.

And I'd hated every fucking minute of it.

But she'd finally texted me late Thursday night. Just a short message, one that had finally allowed me to breathe again.

Sorry about yesterday. Being back here is hard.

That was enough. I'd texted her back immediately, unable to wait another second.

No worries. I'm here if you need me, and I'll be there beside you at the funeral no matter what.

Her smiley face reply with a quick thanks was all I'd needed to calm down and stop being such a cranky bastard, as Gage had called me throughout the day. I'd even headed to bed early after taking a long, hot shower. A shower where I jacked off twice to thoughts of Anabeth kissing me again, of her rubbing that hot little body all over mine. Of taking her to my bed and tasting every inch of her.

Jesus, if I ever got to taste her again, I'd probably come in my pants like a teenager.

But waking up to a text from Finn on Friday—one saying Katie and Anabeth were planning some sort of grand opening celebration for Katie's restaurant and we'd need to work together to help them with setup—sent me right back to that pissed-off place.

Once again, I raced along mountain roads, slipping and sliding through the downpour. This time, I headed to Alder's place. No way was there going to be a party in town without him knowing all the ins and outs of it.

My truck hydroplaned as I hit the end of his driveway, and it was only by sheer, dumb luck that I didn't end up slamming into a tree. Maybe I should have just let the wheel go—let fate or whatever force seemed to drag me through life against the grain of what I thought I wanted take care of everything. But instead, I yanked on the wheel and turned into the skid, waiting for the tires to grab once more before finally hitting the brakes.

I hurried through the rain, pounding across the porch and knocking on the door like my life depended on someone opening it. And I felt like a complete asshole when little Shye answered, her eyes wide and scared.

"What's wrong?"

I shook my head, trying hard to rein in my frustration. "Nothing. I just need to talk to Alder."

She didn't look as if she believed me—I couldn't blame her for that. I was still breathing hard, standing on the doorstep soaking wet. Hell, if she bought my lie, I'd have to think she was stupid. And Shye Anderson was anything but stupid.

"C'mon in," she said, taking a step back. "He's in the shower."

Well, shit. I hadn't thought about the time when I'd rushed over on a workday. "I can come back later. Maybe just see him at the office."

"Don't be silly." She nudged me across the foyer and toward the open kitchen. "Want some coffee? I just brewed a fresh pot for your brother."

"That'd be great. Thanks." I pulled off my coat, frowning down at the puddle I left behind on the pine floors. Shit, how long had I been outside? Long enough to be soaked to the bone, obviously, even though I'd only run from my door to my truck and my truck to Alder's door. This rain seemed endless.

As if Shye knew where my thoughts had gone, she grabbed my coat and headed for the garage. "There's some sweat pants and T-shirts in the laundry room. Help yourself, and I'll hang this up to dry a bit."

"Thank you, Shye."

She shrugged. "We're practically family. That's what family does."

Yeah, it was, but seeing her as family was new for me. Different. Alder had been single a long time, hadn't really dated at all once he'd come back from the Army. But then he'd met Shye, and he hadn't even looked at another woman for three long years as he waited for her to really notice him. I'd mocked him relentlessly about his obsession with her, but honestly? I was sometimes jealous of it. At least he could feel something for a woman. At least he'd gotten to see and talk to her, pine for her while keeping her in his sights. I'd been obsessing over a ghost for more than a decade, one who had run off and started a brand-new life without me. Still was. Likely always would be...and didn't that just piss me right off?

Once I'd changed and tossed my wet clothes into the dryer, I headed back to the kitchen. Shye stood with a mug in her hands, a matching one set in front of one of the stools at the island.

"Thanks for this," I said as I took a seat.

"You looked like you needed something to warm you up."

Warm me up, cool down my temper...I needed all of it.

"Alder said you went to Rock Falls to help set up the funeral arrangements for Miss Hansen."

I clutched the mug as I nodded, letting it warm my cold hands. Giving myself time to settle down a little.

Shye shook her head, looking so very sad. "She was a real nice lady and a good neighbor to me when I lived up on that mountain."

"She was one of a kind and will be missed."

"I met her granddaughter yesterday."

My head snapped up, my attention focused fully on the little blonde across from me. Anabeth had been around town yesterday? "You did?"

"At The Baker's Cottage. She came in for lunch."

Of course—Katie's restaurant would be new, the only big change to Main Street in a long time. Long enough for even Anabeth to realize it was different. Shye had been working at the restaurant a few hours a day to help out. She used to work over at the truck stop on the county line, but Alder hadn't liked her being so far away and unprotected. Not since the Soul Suckers had come for her. Not since we all knew they would again.

God, I hated the fact that Anabeth had been anywhere near the girl. A thought which both surprised me and made me feel like a real dick. It wasn't Shye's fault she had a giant target on her back calling to the men who'd murdered one of our own. But even knowing that, I still didn't want Anabeth around her. Didn't want my girl to run into any danger.

I wanted Anabeth safe, which meant I'd fallen into the well of caring for her. The one I already knew I couldn't get out of.

Motherfucking perfect.

"I think it's great what they're doing," Shye continued, not knowing how much of an ass I felt like all of a sudden. "The email blast Katie sent about the grand opening was really slick and pretty —perfect for her place. Hopefully everyone will show up."

"She sent an email blast?" I hadn't even checked my email this morning. Something I always did. That text from Finn had been the last thing I'd read before jumping into my truck.

"I guess she figured that would be quickest. She's working on a tight time frame to host this thing, what with Anabeth leaving so soon. I mean, if she'd just invited people from Justice, she could have told one of you to get the word out, but she'd wanted to invite people from Rock Falls as well. Spread the net for new customers, you know?"

I did know. And I hated the idea because it would bring outsiders to town. But I couldn't say that to Shye.

Footsteps on the stairs saved me from trying to think up something to say. Alder strolled down to the main level wearing the same sort of baggy gray sweat pants I did, no shirt on, and his hair wet and slightly wavy. He barely even glanced my way before beelining for Shye and wrapping her in a huge hug.

"You made coffee?"

She smiled up at him. "I did. Figured you'd like some before heading out in the rain for the day."

Alder leaned in for a kiss, making me look away as he whispered, "You are so good to me, honey."

For the first time, I felt something hard and dark at seeing the two of them together. Something too close to covetous to ignore. I wanted something like they had—someone to care for and be taken care of by. Someone to come home to other than Gage and his fucking dog.

I wanted a life built on more than one-night stands and work.

"What's up, Bishop?" Alder asked as he let go of Shye and grabbed the mug of coffee she'd poured for him.

"I've got to get ready for work myself. Let me know if you two need anything." Shye left the two of us alone, heading for the stairs as Alder settled in beside me. His eyes tracked her every step, his smile soft and subtle but there. One I hadn't seen on his face before.

"You are so whipped," I said as soon as Shye was out of earshot, pushing back the want and need within me.

"No fucking doubt." He sounded so happy and confident, not the least bit embarrassed about it. "You and Anabeth get all the arrangements made for Miss Hansen?"

"Yeah. Molnar's scheduled a small viewing at the funeral home for tomorrow."

"I'll call him this morning—make sure he knows Kennard Mills will be paying the bill."

"I'm not sure Anabeth will like that idea."

"Don't much care what she likes. She hasn't been here, and Miss Hansen was a pillar of the community. She's ours to take care of all the way into the ground."

There was no arguing with him when he spoke in that tone, so I nodded instead. "You hear about this grand opening Katie's having? Seen the email yet?"

His jaw clenched, his teeth grinding. Yeah, he'd seen it.

"Shye showed me."

"And?"

"I think her uncle's been driving around town a bit too much since she came home, and that he's likely to hear about this party. Might even show up." Her uncle...Sheriff Baker. Even one visit from that jackass was too much. That was definitely something to keep in mind. "And I think two days isn't a lot of time to plan, especially with a funeral tomorrow."

That set me back. "The party is in two days?"

Alder nodded. "That's what the email said. We'll need to set up a perimeter around the building. Make sure we've got all entrances covered with at least two men, plus some inside at all times. This grand opening celebration is going to strain our manpower for sure."

I'd expected him to say he would be putting a stop to it. "You letting Shye work the party?"

Another clench and a jaw tic added in for good measure. "*Let* is not the word I'd use. She's working it, but I'll have a team with her."

"Think the good sheriff will attend?"

If looks could kill, I'd have been nothing but a pile of ash. "He and Katie aren't close, but he might."

"Think the Soul Suckers will show up?"

That question had him sighing. "I know I would if I was looking to make a point."

"Yeah. Me too." I took another drink, plans and operations I'd learned as a SEAL flying through my head. I'd need to pull out some extra firepower, maybe a little more than the standard handgun I carried. It might actually be time to break into some explosives. "I should get back home. Take stock of my supplies in case I need to grab any additional ammunition."

"Good call."

I headed into the laundry room to change, frowning at the dampness of my jeans and the coat I'd retrieved from the garage but knowing I could take a warm shower once I got home. Then I could work out a plan with Gage, and we could start digging through our weapons stash to select the right artillery. Work could wait. No fucking way were the Soul Suckers getting the jump on us.

Alder walked me to the door, frowning at the rain that hadn't eased up in the least. "The flood's going to be bad this year."

"The creek along Widow's Ridge looked ready to overflow this morning. If the dam over the ridge goes, the road won't hold."

"Might be time to move Anabeth into town."

Right. Sure. Easy as wrangling rattlesnakes. "She won't leave that house."

"Then we'd better make sure she has what she needs if the road washes away. At least three days of supplies to get her through. She got a generator?"

"I don't know."

"Ask her. If not, we'll bring up one from the mill."

Right. *Ask her*, as if I spoke to her daily or something. But that request gave me an excuse, plus I'd see her the next day at the funeral. She could *nothing* me all she wanted, I would not be leaving her alone to deal with the death of Miss. "I'll handle it."

Alder raised an eyebrow. Watching me, dissecting me with his eyes. I stayed stoic, military solid and still. Waiting him out. Anabeth wasn't a topic I wanted to discuss—not in light of our kiss, at least. I'd pass on the details of the service and make sure everyone knew we'd lost Miss, but the rest? Me, her, our history, our current situation? No fucking way.

"Whatever you feel is appropriate," my brother finally said, not easing up on his stare for a second. I took that as a win.

I nodded and headed to my truck, ready to get the fuck home. Ex-girlfriends, death of an old friend, a flood, and Soul Suckers. My weekend was quickly shaping up to be the worst one I could remember, which was saying something considering all the hell I'd been through in the SEALs. But all that was nothing it seemed in comparison to rainy season this year.

A flood was coming for me. I just didn't know what part would be more dangerous—the water or the redhead riding the waves.

Chapter Seven

ANABETH

The day before the funeral, Katie showed up on my porch carrying a pie box along with the largest, brightest umbrella I'd ever seen. And it matched her raincoat.

"Good afternoon, Noah," I said, giving her room to come inside. "When you texted that you'd come by today, I expected you to show up with your menagerie of animals marching inside two by two."

Her grin positively sparkled. "Aw, bible humor from the local witch. How quaint."

"Trust me, if I were a witch, I'd be casting spells to end the rain." I frowned at the too-dark sky. "John Molnar called to warn me that the funeral might be pretty empty because of the weather."

"I figured as much. People are nervous. You missed the floods of 2012. We lost four houses that year." She handed me the pie box with a smile. "For you. I remember you used to like the peach tarts my mom made, and this is the closest thing to those that I do."

"Peach pie?"

"Better."

I opened the lid, groaning when the smells of sugar and cinnamon and peach washed over me. "Cobbler."

"Yup. Old-school and totally not fancy, but delicious and perfect for eating your feelings." She hung up her coat and removed her boots, offering me a half smile when she was done. "New day, new feelings. How are you doing?"

I shrugged because, really... How could I answer that?

Katie didn't seem to need more, though. "My favorite memory of Miss was from an elementary school bake sale when I was in first grade. She brought in these cookies with Miss Piggy faces painted on them in icing. But she'd had the heat too high on the way to Rock Falls, and the icing had melted so they looked like horrible pink monsters instead. And when she saw them, she looked right at me, held one up, and said, 'Remember, little one. Always eat the bad guys before they eat you.' And then she ate that horrible, monster-faced cookie with a smile."

I laughed, hard and loud and strong right there in the foyer of the house where Miss had just recently died. "That sounds exactly like something she would have done. I love it, thank you for sharing that story with me."

"You're welcome. Now, tell me really—how are you holding up? What can I do to help?"

That was easy enough. I'd been alone in the house too much, enough that a chat with an old friend sounded like heaven. "Have a cup of tea with me, and let's go over grand opening details. I need a distraction."

Katie's smile widened. "Done."

I led her to the kitchen, still basking in the warmth her story had brought me. It truly did sound exactly like something Miss would have done—taken a bad situation and made it better. She'd done that by taking me in. She'd done it a second time by sending me to Vegas to live with a friend of hers who worked the Strip as a medium. She'd continued doing it by accepting that I wouldn't come back and spending every vacation in Vegas with me. She was a fixer even when she didn't know how to fix something. I would truly miss her.

"Are these your cards?" Katie asked, staring down at the tarot spread I'd been pulling when she rang the bell.

"Sure are."

"Is it true you only use the one deck?"

"How did you—"

"You did that interview on the Vegas morning channel last year." She shrugged, nudging a card with the very tip of her finger. "I watched it on YouTube."

Of course she did. "Ah, well yes, that's true. Miss bought me these cards when I came to live with her and showed an interest in them. It's the only deck I use, and we work well together."

"The cards work with you?"

"Absolutely. Decks have personalities. In fact, Miss used to have a deck that hated men. Every time she tried to read for a guy, the cards would only show death, destruction, and humiliation. It was funny, really. Taught me a lot about how to manipulate a card to mess with someone's head." I nodded toward the spread of cards on the counter. "Would you like me to read for you?"

"Oh, no. That's not why I came here."

But she couldn't stop looking at the cards, so I picked them up and shuffled, sensing her interest. "How about one card? A quick and dirty read of your life." I fanned the deck in my hands and leaned toward her. "Pick one. Just one."

Katie bit her lip before focusing on the cards. It took her a good fifteen seconds to choose the card she wanted and pull it from the deck.

"It's my first time." She handed the card to me with a cautious smile. "Be gentle."

"I'm always gentle."

The card staring back at me featured a couple holding hands, with an older woman watching over them. I raised my eyebrows as I looked back at Katie. "Are you in a relationship?"

"Nope," she said. "Single as the day is long."

"That long day is coming to a close. You pulled the lovers." I tucked the card back into the deck. "The lovers card symbolizes choice—you, not being in a relationship, will have the choice soon to grow into one. To pick a partner and join your souls so they're no longer two separate entities, but three counting the combined one. It's a good card."

"Does it say who that partner will be?"

"No, I'm sorry. That would have been more Miss' skill than mine."

Just saying her name, remembering all the times she'd tell me about the souls and the spirits and the cards themselves, made my heart hurt again. I hadn't gotten enough time with her. Not nearly enough minutes to simply talk and tell stories. But she was gone, and I would never get another chance.

"Maybe this new man will show up at the party. Which reminds me," Katie started as she settled at the little table by the window, pulling me from my thoughts of Miss and loss. Thank goodness. "I was thinking I'd serve small plates." She held up her hand as I opened my mouth to argue. "I know with the type of guys they grow here in Justice, you'll say I should serve full portions. But I really think if they try more than one or two things, I'll make a better impression. I can make like eight entrees, four soups, and three desserts. Keep the plates small but constant so they eat throughout the event."

Huh. That wasn't what I would have done, and yet... "It sounds perfect. They'll only get grumbly about the size of the portion with the first plate."

"Right, plus I can put full-size portions on display in the dessert case so they know exactly what they'd get with a regular order."

I handed her a cup of steaming water and laid my collection of teas in front of her before taking a seat. "You are brilliant. All the men in town will quickly fall under the spell of your delicious food and offer their undying affection for your hand."

"Lord, I wish. Not to be blunt, but I've been in a bit of a dry spell lately."

Okay. So...we were going there. "Sometimes a break is good."

"A three-year break? No. That's not good. It's practically sadistic."

I hadn't had sex in far longer than three years, but I wasn't about to tell her that. "Anyone caught your eye?"

She looked away, blushing. "I mean... I've had a crush on Bishop practically since birth."

The world went gray, and my breath caught. Oh God, if she told me she was dating him, that she'd had sex with him...that she had fallen in love with my...my...

I couldn't even think it.

"Oh." I stared down into my tea, unable to come up with more words.

Katie just laughed, though. "My God, quit looking like I just kicked your puppy. I would never try to date him—there's no way I'd be able to fill your shoes there. Besides, Bishop doesn't date."

"What do you mean, he doesn't date?"

"Just what I said—the man doesn't date. Hasn't since he came home from the military as far as I know. At least, that's what Mercy told me."

"Military?" Bishop was in the military? Mercy...Mercy...that sounded so familiar. "And who's Mercy?"

"You don't remember her? Her family owns the hardware store in town. She dated—"

"Finn." Of course—Mercy Bell. Finn's girlfriend his senior year of high school. She hadn't liked me much, probably because of how close I was with her man. But Finn and I had been friends for years at that point. He was the one who'd introduced me to his brother.

"Mercy's still here? I thought she had plans to go to college after high school."

"She did, but like a lot of us, she came back. She got some sort of business degree online and runs the hardware store for her dad now. And she has a kid."

That... Wow. That news hit me harder than it should have. My heart stuttered, and a wave of something close to jealousy washed over me. "Is it Finn's?"

"Oh, gosh no. She left him long before that. I don't even think they made it to graduation."

Yeah, neither had I. After I'd found out about Finn and the drugs, after everything that happened that spring, I'd skipped out of town without even finishing my senior year. Miss had sent me to Vegas, knowing I needed a different scene, but she'd demanded I get my GED or she'd drag my ass back to Justice to deal with everything head on. I hadn't been ready to do that, so I'd followed her direction, earning my GED before that first summer had ended, even completing a tech school program to become a dental hygienist. I'd never needed it, though. Once I'd earned that first dollar reading tea leaves, I'd known I'd found my calling.

Sadly, it had been without Bishop by my side. Back then, before everything had gone to shit, I'd wanted to marry Bishop Kennard. He'd stolen my heart slowly, breaking down walls I hadn't even known I'd built up with his charm and kindness, the way he evoked feelings within me. Giving me that smile that I felt in my knees. And if I was being honest with myself, he still held a big chunk of my heart. A chunk I knew I'd never get back.

"As much as I hate to do it so soon, I should get going." Katie stood suddenly, yanking me from my nostalgia. "I've got pies to bake and prep work to do. Oh, speaking of which, I'll be bringing little things to nosh on to the funeral, so don't agree to Molnar's jacked-up prices for any of that."

I followed her down the hall toward the foyer. "You have your party the next night. I can't ask you to make food."

"You're not. I'm basically inserting myself into your life and forcing you to accept it."

Her sweetness was going to make me cry. "Thank you. I greatly appreciate it, and I'd be happy to pay you instead of Molnar. I'm sure your food will be better anyway."

"Don't worry about it. I already let the Kennards know they'd be getting a bill."

My back went stiff. "Pardon?"

She paused, raincoat half on, surprise evident on her face. "This is Justice, Anabeth. The Kennards pay for every funeral. It's tradition."

Of course they would. "Fine. Then I'm refusing payment for the tarot card reading at your event." I held up my finger, this time stopping her. "Don't even think about arguing. I wasn't going to accept it anyway."

She shrugged her coat on, giving me a solidly fake glare. "You drive a hard bargain."

"Never mess with a Vegas performer. We know where they hide the bodies."

Katie laughed and tugged on her boots before giving me a hug. "It was good to see you. Call me if you need anything, okay?"

"I will." I wouldn't, but she probably knew that.

As I opened the door for her, the wind blew, and the view to the woods cleared for just a moment. Long enough to see a glimpse of a shadow that shouldn't have been there. I stared hard, trying to see it again, but the rain made everything blurry and indistinct. Either that, or being alone in the house so much had started a sort of weird paranoia in me. All those stories of the Soul Suckers definitely weren't helping.

Once Katie had driven down the driveway and turned onto the road, I shut the door. I locked it, too. Not my usual habit out here, but something that seemed like the right thing to do. The ticking of the clock in the living room seemed too loud—gunshots in the dimming daylight—and the house suddenly felt almost oppressive. Too big, too empty. Too many memories of all the things I'd given up along the way. Or lost.

God, so much loss.

I was back in the kitchen making another cup of tea when the feeling of being watched washed over me. I glanced at my phone on the counter, remembering how Bishop had said to call him if anything seemed wrong, but I didn't reach for it. Not yet, at least. I was an independent woman who'd lived on her own for years in a bigger, meaner city than Justice would ever be. So instead, I walked over to the windows, looking out into the rainy gloom of the early evening.

Nothing to see but water.

"Stupid, silly girl." Still, the feeling refused to let me go. Anxious, scattered, and slightly jumpy, I nearly screamed when the kettle began to whistle. I rushed to the stove to turn the burner off with shaking hands. "You're being ridiculous."

Instead of feeding into the silly fear making my heart pound, I poured the water into my tea press, watching the leaves dance over the little filter. Starting to count to get just the right brew. When I reached the two-minute mark, I poured the tea into my mug before turning around. The deck of tarot cards called to me, sitting there all neat and tidy. Waiting for me to pull and read them.

"Just one," I said, reaching for the deck and giving myself over to my instincts. I pulled a single card, one that sent a shiver up my spine, before turning it around.

Death.

I never liked pulling the death card during a reading because most people reacted to the name and didn't listen to the truth behind it. The death card didn't signify a loss of life—it meant an end to something. A phase of transition. In the picture on the face, the sky was not completely black but gray, and the sun had not yet set. It was a card that spoke of a definitive ending and a time of significant transformation. It signified the death of the way things had been and the possibilities of a new future.

The only thought in my head as I stared at that card was Bishop. My relationship with him. Our past. I'd never told him why I left. Maybe that's what the card meant. An opening up of my soul for Bishop to judge. An ending to missing him and wanting him back.

A true ending to our relationship.

That thought had me tossing the card toward the rest of the deck and stepping away from the counter...

And promptly spilling hot tea all over myself when I saw a man's face staring back at me through the kitchen window.

Chapter Eight

BISHOP

The planning session for how we'd handle Miss' funeral and the grand opening at The Baker's Cottage ran a lot longer than I'd expected. Alder had wanted Camden involved, even though his drinking had gotten a bit out of control. I figured my brother assumed keeping a solid eye on Camden would help him somehow. I also figured Camden showed up to make Alder happy, but that he didn't want to be there. He sat at the back of the room, silent, curled in on himself. Not interacting with anyone. The man was a walking train wreck, and I didn't know how to help him. If we could at all.

"What about the rain?" Jackson, the mill's lead silviculturist—the guy who made sure we left the forests we harvested healthier than when we started working there—hollered from the back after Alder had laid out plans for coverage, protection, and shift changes.

Every eye in the room locked in on my brother. The rain, and the possibility of flooding, seemed to be a much bigger worry to the town than the Soul Suckers, something I normally would have agreed with...except there was a red-haired woman I couldn't keep my mind off of. One who lived all alone in a house on a ridge right in the middle of the shitstorm the Soul Suckers had started. Even though she wanted nothing from me, she had somehow become my biggest worry.

"Wear protective gear and watch for cars or trucks you don't recognize at either site. These guys won't be driving in on bikes. I also want eyes watching for the sheriff. We need to know if he crosses into town as well," Alder said, his voice leaving no room for argument. "I know we've got issues right now with the rain, guys. But Anabeth and Katie need this, so we're going to pull through for them. Once we put Miss Hansen in the ground tomorrow and get through this grand opening thing the next night, we can focus on the flooding. Because it will flood—there's no doubt. Two creeks have already spilled over."

The guys all mumbled agreements, talking softly to one another as Alder ended the meeting and sent us on our way. My way happened to overlap with Gage's, seeing as he was staying at my house. I hadn't talked to him much in the last few days. Somewhat intentionally.

"You never told me about Anabeth," Gage said as we reached my truck. Starting the conversation I knew he'd want to have. He hopped into the passenger side, Rex jumping in right after him to settle at his feet. The beast brought quite the aroma of wet dog with him. My truck would reek of that for days. A small irritation in comparison to how I felt talking about Anabeth to anyone, including my best friend.

"Wasn't much to tell."

"Bullshit."

Totally. "She was my girlfriend when I was in college."

"Finn said you wanted to marry her."

I'd bought a ring and everything, but that wasn't anyone's

business. And I was going to kill my brother. "I did. At one time. But that didn't work out."

"Too bad. She's got killer legs."

The truck lurched to the side as I spun toward him, thankfully not sending us careening off the road. "What does that have to do with anything?"

If that bastard thought for one second he could make a play for my girl...

"Nothing," he said, shrugging and looking like he'd just pulled one over on me. Which he likely had. "I just really wanted to comment on her legs."

To get a rise out of me. The asshole. Not that I wouldn't have done the same thing to him. "That mutt is going to make my truck stink."

"Don't take out your anger on Rex, man. It's not his fault you can't climb between those long, soft legs again."

Without taking my eyes off the road, I punched him in the shoulder. He just grunted and laughed. He didn't push, though. Didn't poke or prod me for more information. He accepted what I said and what I didn't without judgment. Like a good friend would.

We made it to my place quickly enough, each jumping out of the truck and walking the perimeter of the house once I'd parked. We didn't need directions or plans—we'd done this a million times while serving together and since he'd moved to Justice. Verifying a location's security was practically habit.

Once we'd met back up at the front porch, I took my phone out of my pocket and followed Gage as he opened the door. I still needed to check my work emails before I could call it a day, and I had a serious need to call Anabeth. Just to check on her. Make sure she was okay. Because I was a huge sucker when it came to that girl. Maybe I'd do that last so I wouldn't feel like such a needy little prick. Maybe I'd do it first to get it over with.

Fuck, when did dealing with women get so difficult?

The text alert on my phone went off as I stepped inside. I nearly smiled when I saw Anabeth's name on my screen. Maybe she'd been thinking of me as much as I'd been thinking of her. She'd reached out—that had to be a good sign. More than the *nothing* she'd claimed to have wanted from me.

I swiped faster than normal, annoyingly excited at the thought that she'd missed me. But the moment I read her message, the roaring of my blood pounding in my ears nearly drowned out everything else. Not a good sign. Not at all.

"What is it?" Gage asked, looking more than just a little concerned. I tossed him the phone as I rushed to the closet where I'd been keeping a small bag of supplies—night vision goggles, a few select guns, ammunition, and a couple of grenades—in case I needed to go hard and fast.

Anabeth's short, simple message of *there's a man outside watching me* meant I needed to go as hard and fast as possible.

"Motherfucker," Gage said with a growl in his voice. I felt no need to respond—that was an understatement, and he knew it.

"You carrying?" I sighted down my favorite pistol—a Colt M1911 semiautomatic—and tucked it into my shoulder holster before tossing the bag over my shoulder.

"Always. Let's go." Gage whistled to Rex as I raced out into the rain, slamming the door closed behind him and following me to my truck. We were back inside the cab and screaming down the road within seconds, but it still wasn't fast enough. Nothing would have been fast enough, considering. And the fucking rain making the roads slick and the drive more treacherous than usual certainly wasn't helping.

"She's all alone up there," I said before slamming my fist against the wheel as I once again had to slow down for a curve.

Gage stared out the windshield, focused and solid. "We'll get there."

My heart leaped as I curled my hand into a fist again. Yeah, we'd get there. Except he'd said the same thing when we'd heard Camden's house was burning and were trying hard to get there in time. That hadn't turned out so well for the woman inside the house...or the man who loved her.

"Plan?" Gage asked as I made the turn onto the road leading to Widow's Ridge. Water from the creek flowed over part of it, but I flew through the mess, gripping the wheel tight as I lost traction. Another couple inches, and that section would likely be impassible. But not yet. Didn't matter if I hydroplaned all the way to that old farmhouse—I *would* be getting up that fucking road.

Once my tires gripped hard ground again, I hit the gas and roared up the steep, gravel path to the Hansen place. "I'll secure Anabeth. You watch my back and do a preliminary perimeter check in case I need to pull her out." I shook my head, unable to stop thinking of the worst. Of Leah and that fire. Of Anabeth burning. "I'm going in no matter what."

Gage grunted, probably thinking the same thoughts I was. Remembering the same night. And knowing, no matter how hot things were about to get, I was going after my girl.

"We'll get her out," he said roughly before thumping the dashboard with his fist. "No matter what, we'll get her out of there."

Yeah, we would. The only question was if she would be alive and whole when we pulled her out or not.

But as we crested the last hill before her place, I spotted the house through the trees. No smoke. No fire. The relief at that fact was almost enough to make me relax.

Almost.

"Get ready," I told Gage, not that I needed to. He'd already taken off his seat belt and was sitting almost sideways on the seat, hand on the door handle, ready to rush into the fight.

As soon as I came to a stop in Anabeth's driveway, I threw my door open and jumped out of the truck, not even bothering to pull my keys from the ignition. My feet slipped in the mud on my way to her door, but I pushed through. Running hard, racing toward the porch and praying with everything I had that she was okay. That the house was still secure and she was inside alone.

Anabeth opened the door as I hit the porch, looking pale and shaky. Terrified. And in that moment, something broke inside of me. Something that had been holding me back. Something that made me understand how much this woman still meant to me and always would.

I lifted her up in a hug as I rushed inside, pulling her right off her feet and holding her tightly to my chest. "You okay?"

She clung to me, trembling. "Yeah, just...uneasy."

Thank the fucking stars. I set her down on her feet again, knowing I needed to get to work. "All right, then. We're going to check things out. Where'd you see him?"

"Through the kitchen window."

Backside of the house. That would help us narrow our search. "Stay right here and lock up after me."

But the blatant fear on her face killed me. I couldn't leave her that way. Without a second thought, I leaned down and pressed my lips to hers, sliding my tongue into her mouth when she gasped and kissing her with everything I had. Everything I needed. Everything I'd fucking missed for the last fourteen years. I kissed her with my heart and soul on my sleeve, and she responded just as strong. As deep. Wrapping her arms around my neck and holding me against her. Slipping her tongue against mine and moaning softly when I grabbed her ass to get a better hold on her. To change my angle so I could own that damn kiss.

She'd initiated the kiss in her driveway, but this time, it was all me. All my needs and wants. I laid everything out with that kiss. Bared my soul through action and not words. But I had to break the connection, had to get to work. Because someone had been stupid enough to come for my girl, and that couldn't be ignored.

"I have to go," I murmured against her lips, stealing one more peck before letting her go. "Stay inside and lock the fucking door. Gage and I will be back as soon as we check the perimeter."

Anabeth nodded, her lips dark pink and swollen from my kiss. Her eyes a little more hooded and a lot less afraid. Good. Just what I wanted.

Anxious to get this over with, I grabbed my pistol from my shoulder holster and ran back outside to find and kill the fucker who had dared to threaten her with his presence. Gage stood on the front steps, looking out into the rain with his gun drawn and ready.

"You've got the wrong shoes on for this," he said, not looking over his shoulder at me. Not needing to.

Again with my fucking shoes, though he wasn't wrong. My feet were already soaked. "I'll deal. She saw him through the kitchen window, which is at the back. Let's do this."

I followed Gage off the porch and into the rain. We crept around the house quickly, our guns drawn and Rex slinking along at our heels. The evening had fallen fast, the clouds blocking out the last of the sunlight, so there wasn't much to see. Shadows upon shadows—no footprints, no trespasser, no sign of anything wrong. At least, not until we hit the back porch.

"Mud," Gage said, pointing his gun at the spots leading to the kitchen window...and then past it to the back door. The screen sat open an inch or so, and there was what looked like a wet handprint on the glass in the door itself. I stared at that print, seeing exactly what had happened—right hand on the glass to push, left working the knob to release the latch. The old door wasn't steel or reinforced, and the lockset had definitely seen better days. One good shoulder bump was all it would have taken. And my guess was, the fucker knew it.

"He tried to get in." My blood roiled, crashing into my heart with every pump.

Gage grunted. "But he didn't force it. Why not? A woman home alone would have been easy prey. What made him stop?"

Prey. My girl as prey. I stared at that door, at that handprint, trying to work it out myself. Trying to think like a sick, soulless criminal.

Like the kind of bastards who would set a house on fire knowing a woman slept inside it.

"Orders," I said, the pieces falling together in my mind. "He wasn't here for her. He had other orders."

"Even orders won't stop someone forever." Gage looked out past the porch into the dark, rainy night. "We need to search the woods."

"We *need* to get a team up here first. We can't search and keep Anabeth safe."

He didn't challenge me, knowing I was right. Probably also knowing there was no fucking way I was leaving her alone right then. The need to protect her overrode my desire to find the bastard who'd been watching. Who'd had an opportunity to do some serious damage but didn't take it.

We wouldn't get that lucky twice.

I led the way back around the house, getting wetter by the second. I stopped and checked every window for any signs of tampering, hoping like hell this guy would pop out of the dark so I could take care of him. No dice, though. Fucking coward had probably either run or hidden when he saw us pull up, if he'd still been on the property at all. A thought which sent my mind spinning. How long had he watched Anabeth? How many windows had he peeped through? And how likely was he to come back and disobey whatever orders he'd been following?

Likely, was my guess. Very likely. Which meant we couldn't just let him disappear into the woods without a chase.

We reached the front porch in almost no time, both of us soaked to the skin and probably looking like drowned rats. Not that it mattered—even the cold couldn't get to me in that moment. I had enough rage and fear running through my body to keep me warm. I also had a woman on the other side of the door who needed me to protect her. A little water wouldn't stop me from that, but we definitely needed backup.

"Call my brother. Get his ass up here," I said to Gage as I knocked on the front door. Anabeth opened it slowly, looking behind me before pulling it wide. Smart girl. "He was on your back porch. We're calling for backup before we go into the woods to track him. Have you been out there today?"

Her hands shook, and she seemed to grow even paler. "I never go into those woods."

That struck me as off—she used to. Back when we were together, we'd spent many an afternoon out in those woods. We'd had our first kiss out there, had lost our virginity to each other out there. She'd loved exploring them then. And me. And us. Something had changed, but I didn't have the time to figure out what just then.

"Good. Stay out of them unless I'm with you, okay?"

She looked us up and down, her eyes going wide as she took a step back. "You're soaked. Get in here and warm up."

I shook my head. "We'll make a mess if we—"

"Bishop Kennard, get your ass in this house and out of the rain. You too, Gage. Please."

The two of us stepped inside as she disappeared down the hall. She came back a few seconds later holding a towel in each hand.

"Here," she said. "I don't have any clothes that might fit you, but you can at least dry off a little."

"Thanks." I ran the towel over my hair, scrubbing hard to pull as much water out as possible. Gage did the same, though he had a lot more hair to deal with.

"Bishop," Anabeth whispered once I dropped my arm, her eyes locked on me. Her hands clasped together. She nearly vibrated with tension, with a need for something I couldn't quite put my finger on. At least not until she inched forward. Staring at my chest. At my arms.

"I'm soaked. I'll make you wet and cold if I hold you right now."

Anabeth shook her head, still unable to meet my eyes. "I don't care."

Then I didn't either. I tugged her back into my arms, wrapping myself around her as best I could. Holding her tightly. And fuck, did it feel good to have her body pressed against mine. To know she looked to me to comfort her in such a scary moment.

"I've got you, Anabeth. Nothing's going to happen with me here." I turned to Gage, not letting go of her. "You get ahold of Alder?"

Gage stared back at me with a hard expression on his face. "Roger that. He's four minutes out."

A man could make it pretty far in four minutes, but there was no way I was leaving Anabeth alone while Gage and I went hunting in the woods. That was a fool's mission—something inexperienced fucks would do. We weren't inexperienced.

"How about you turn the lights off on this level?" I said. "We don't want anyone to have an advantage on us."

Gage disappeared without a word, flicking off lights as he went stomping through the house. I stayed with Anabeth secure in my hold. Unable to let her go. Not wanting to either.

"I don't understand what's happening," she said, her forehead resting against my chest and her hands clutching my wet shirt.

"My guess is the Soul Suckers came out here to see what was going on, and someone spotted you. Maybe decided to get a closer look." I squeezed her tighter when she stiffened. "Don't worry. We'll take care of them."

"But...how? And why would they be out on the ridge? I can't imagine Miss did anything to them."

I didn't know how to tell her about the meth lab on her property, so I was thankful when headlights danced across the wall. Gage slipped into place beside the window, moving the curtain just enough to see out to the driveway. "Alder's here."

Time to get back to work.

I squeezed Anabeth one last time, then let her go. She shivered and wrapped her arms around herself, so I draped my towel around her and gave her a quick kiss on the forehead.

"Told you I'd make you cold."

She shot me one hell of a beautiful half smile. "Worth it."

Yeah, it was.

Shaking my head, trying to clear it of thoughts of what else would be worth it right about then, I headed to open the front door. My brother hurried in a moment later, his gun drawn, Camden right behind him.

Camden looked like hell.

"You look like shit on toast, man," Gage said, apparently reading my mind.

"Have a twenty-year relationship with someone and then deal with their murder, jackass. We'll see who looks better. Until then, shut the fuck up."

The entire room went still and silent. I glanced at Alder, letting him figure out how to handle this new, uncharacteristically angry Camden.

Luckily, my brother didn't have any hesitancy about handling shit. "Knock it off, Cam. We're a team, so fucking act like it. Now, we need one man in the house with Anabeth, the rest in the woods." He held my gaze, giving me the option. Letting me know it would be okay if I decided to hang back. But I wanted to get my hands dirty, wanted to wring the neck of the man who'd scared my girl. Wanted it badly enough to trust her safety to a friend.

"Camden stays. I'm hunting."

"Done, then." Alder pulled a pair of night vision goggles from inside his coat. "Let's suit up."

"Wait," Anabeth said as I pulled my own goggles over my head. "You can't go out there. What if he has a gun?"

I shrugged. "Mine's bigger."

"This isn't funny." Her voice rose, and she looked close to panicking again. "You can't go out there. You're a marketing executive."

I...had no idea what the fuck one had to do with the other. Gage seemed to, though.

"He's also a retired Navy SEAL, as am I. Alder was Special Forces, and Camden was a Marine. Some jackass playing Peeping Tom isn't going to get the jump on us, so why don't you sit back and let us handle this, Legs. We need a little fun now and again."

Anabeth recoiled. "Did he just call me Legs?"

"Yeah, but they really are great legs. It had to be said." I ignored my asshole best friend and grabbed her hand, smiling when she gave me an exasperated look. "We've got this. It'll be okay."

She leaned closer and lowered her voice. "I never knew you wanted to join the military."

Of course not, because it hadn't crossed my mind until she'd left me. The fact that we'd lost so many years together—that we didn't know each other's lives as well as we once had—slammed into me with those words. Might as well start to right that particular ship immediately. "I hadn't ever really thought about it, but after..."

I couldn't finish my sentence, couldn't mention that I'd joined right after she'd left me. Right after I'd hunted her down in Vegas, only to find her living in some cheap-ass apartment off the Strip with an older man. Right after Alder had come to pick me up and cart my sorry ass home, bitching the entire time about all the shit he should have been doing with his unit instead of dealing with me and my broken heart. His words had stuck with me, his sense of duty to others making an impression.

And Anabeth knew none of that. "When did you join?"

"Bishop, let's go." Gage pounded on the doorjamb, waiting for me. Alder stood at his side watching me. Waiting.

Shit.

I looked back to Anabeth, not having the time to make up a lie. Not wanting to either. "I came back from Vegas—from looking for you—on a Wednesday. I was at the recruiter's office that Monday."

A look of pain flashed across her face, the force of which nearly knocked me over. But I had shit to do—things that took priority over rehashing decisions I couldn't change. Decisions I was actually proud of, even if they'd started off because of what she'd done.

"It's not a bad thing," I said quietly, cupping her face and running my thumb along her lips. "We can talk about it later, okay? First, I have to take care of this guy for you."

I let her go and turned to leave, but she dove for me. Forced me to turn back around. Grabbed me by the shoulders and crashed her lips to mine and stole one hell of a good, long kiss before finally letting me go.

"Be careful."

I wanted to tell *her* that—to be careful with those kisses. With that curvy body of hers and the way she pressed herself against me. But if the way she eyed me as she took a step backward was any indication, she knew exactly what she was doing to me. And hopefully, she'd do it again when we didn't have company.

Chapter Nine

ANABETH

I paced. What else could I do? Bishop had gone out into the woods, into the dark, to hunt down whoever had been watching me through the window. True, he had much more training for such things than I'd ever thought possible, but still...he was likely putting himself in danger for me.

And honestly, the fact that he'd joined the Navy after I'd left him—become a SEAL. That was hard to reconcile with the younger Bishop I'd fallen in love with. I knew Alder had become a Green Beret during the last year Bishop and I'd been together, but I'd never known exactly what those soldiers did. A SEAL? Everyone knew the sort of stuff they did. That job was so dangerous. And sexy. My god, was it sexy.

"Can you stop pacing, please?" Camden said, looking like the biggest grump in the world. Not at all how I remembered him, though I figured that was to be expected. Leah had been alive then and wasn't anymore. I couldn't even imagine the pain he had to be feeling at her loss.

"Sorry." I fidgeted for a few more minutes, staring out at the darkness on the other side of the window. Waiting. Forever waiting. "Want to pull a card or two?"

Camden frowned. "What?"

"Cards." I grabbed my tarot deck from the bookshelf. "Tarot cards. Reading them soothes me."

He shrugged one shoulder. "Whatever."

I shuffled the cards, focusing on Camden and letting the energy pass between us before holding out the deck to him. "Think of the present, of right now, and pick one card."

Camden looked doubtful, but he did as I asked. At least, the picking part. "It's a witch."

I frowned as he turned the card. "It's a hermit, not a witch. She indicates a time of isolation and loneliness, of pulling away from others."

He grunted, staring at the card in his hand. "Looks like a witch to me."

Okay, then. "This time, think about your future when you pull a card. About things to come."

He looked at me as if I was crazy but pulled a card anyway. "People waving."

"Four of Wands. A card symbolizing a homecoming, a new start. That's a lovely one. Pull another."

This time, he almost seemed wary. Nervous. Afraid to touch the deck, but he pushed past all that and grabbed a single card, handing it to me before he even looked. On the card face, two children stood outside what looked like a home. One sniffed a bouquet of flowers while the other looked up at what was presumably their sibling. It was a good card, a happy one.

Unless your wife had just been murdered or you'd lost something else as precious along the way in life.

My voice sounded weak as I said, "Six of Cups."

"What's it mean?"

I bit my lip, unsure how to word this. How to give him hope without drowning him in the inevitable guilt of the meaning behind it.

"A new start." I turned the card so he could see. "The smaller child represents the past while the taller one represents the future. Together, they indicate happy reunions with past friends or lovers." I pointed to a figure in the background. "See the man walking away? That's your worries leaving you to be locked away for storage. Never forgotten, just…put somewhere they can't hurt you anymore."

"What else?" His words came out as a growl, his eyes hardening and his body stiff. There was no backing out, though. No way to lie to him.

"The house symbolizes security and comfort, but the garden is barren, see? That's a nod to the lost times of the past. Moments never to be had again. But overall, it's a happy card. One filled with hope."

Camden stared at the card for a long minute, darting his eyes back and forth as he absorbed every detail. And then he handed it back.

"Bullshit. I've seen the crap you pull in Vegas—you're only giving me that new start line because you already know about Leah."

"Camden, I'm not—"

"Drop it, red. There is no hope for me."

Before I could even think of a reply, Gage opened the front door and stormed inside with Alder on his heels. The dog, too.

"Everything okay in here?" Alder asked, looking between Camden and me. I shrugged, shrinking under the glare Gage sent me. The man scared me to no end, and I had a feeling he didn't like me. I just didn't know why.

"Find anything?" Camden stood and headed for Alder. If I hadn't known better, I'd have said he was interested in the mission the other men had completed. But I did know—I knew exactly how to keep people from seeing your pain and trying to dig down deep. To keep them from attempting to get to the bottom of it.

For some hurts, there was no bottom to the ache, and for some people, distraction came as easily as a question and an interested expression.

"Nothing but footprints. Someone was definitely out there." Alder looked my way. "I'm going to need you to move out of this house and come stay with one of us."

Statement dropped. No question. No option. No choice. Screw that.

"No. This is Miss' house, and I want to stay here."

Bishop slipped in behind his brother, looking so very dangerous with his hair soaked and his dark goggles on top of his head. "We'll handle it."

Alder looked from me to him before nodding. "If you think that's best."

"Wait," I said. "If what's best? How are you handling it?"

Bishop glared, something mean and dark in his eyes. Something not directed at me. "You can't be alone. There was a man in your woods—on your fucking porch—watching you. We've already suffered a loss because of these assholes. Either you move in to town with us, or we move in to this house with you. Take your pick, but those are your only choices."

And there it was—that Kennard bossiness. Still, the idea of moving was simply too reprehensible to consider. "Fine. I stay."

"Then Gage and I move in."

"Make it happen," Alder said. "And make sure she has all our contact numbers, just in case."

Bishop nodded, shooting me a heated look before following Alder and Camden out the door. Leaving me with Gage. And his dog.

"I need some tea," I said, unbalanced after all the fear and the new information and the time spent with Camden. I probably needed something stronger, but I didn't drink.

"Mind making me a cup?"

I blinked, taken by surprise. "Sure. I'd be happy to."

Gage followed me around the kitchen, silent and stealthy. Predator-like. I could practically feel his eyes on me, sense his hungry gaze. I didn't like it.

My hands shook as I pulled my tea box out. "Green tea okay?"

"Whatever." Yeah, he wasn't a tea drinker, which meant he had another reason for hanging with me in the kitchen.

I set the kettle to boil and opened my tea box, fiddling with the bags and lining them up just so. Taking up time until I had to turn around and face the man behind me. Thankfully, Bishop rushed in at that moment and broke the tension.

"Hey," he said as he hurried over. He didn't give me the opportunity to do much more than smile before he grabbed me and yanked me into another huge, wet hug. One that felt so good, I almost wanted to cry. My god, had I ever missed him. Missed this.

"Are you all right?" I asked, so glad he'd made it back to me in one piece.

"I should be asking you that." He pulled back and ran a finger down my cheek, his brow furrowed. "Are you okay with this?"

I shrugged, unsure.

His worried look softened, and he tugged me again. Dragging me to him with a small smile on his face. "I just want you safe, Firefly."

Every wall I'd ever built crumbled. He used to call me that, back before I left. Back before I'd ruined everything. He'd called me Firefly, and hearing that word from his lips again melted my heart in ways nothing else could have.

I stepped into his body, wrapping my arms around his waist and letting him hold me. Allowing myself to relax against him and remember—truly remember. Not just the big moments or the happy times, but all of it. The arguing, the exploring, the good times, and the bad. The moments that tested us and taught us. The ones that consumed us. First times and last and everything in between. I remembered, and I craved. I knew I couldn't get that back, but my god, did I want to try.

I didn't leave his hold until the kettle whistled, drawing my attention away from my first and only love. I turned to shut off the flame and caught Gage's glare. Hard and deadly. He stared at me as if I was the enemy, the villain in his story. Or maybe in Bishop's.

"I need to run to my house to grab some supplies," Bishop said, heading toward the table where Gage sat. "Want me to grab your jump bag?"

"Yeah. And your extra phone charger. I lost my last one and haven't replaced it yet."

"What's a jump bag?" I asked, setting the tea to steep.

"A bag we keep packed and at the ready for moments like this. Otherwise, we'd either both have to leave, or I'd have to dig through Gage's underwear drawer. And that's a nightmare I don't intend to live out." Bishop laughed and smacked Gage on the arm before heading for the door. "Eyes up, man."

"I've got this." Gage watched his friend leave before turning back to me. The smile there, the warmth he'd shown Bishop, disappeared in a heartbeat, leaving me with a wild animal filled with some sort of rage.

I needed to find firmer footing with him. "How old is your dog?"

"Don't know. Found him on the side of the road a few years back. Someone had left him like he was garbage, giving him up and running away instead of taking care of him as they should. People are assholes, you know?"

His words...hurt. Hitting home in a way I had no doubt he'd intended.

"You're a good man for taking care of him," I said, my voice rougher than I would have liked. Softer too. Gage simply stared back, his eyes flat. Waiting for me to make a mistake. Until he couldn't wait anymore, it seemed.

"Bishop never mentioned you."

I blinked, nodding as I looked down at my mug. "I'm not really surprised by that."

But I was, and he knew it.

"I am. You see, when a man doesn't give a shit, he talks like it's his job. Words come easy, stories have a way of telling themselves, and bullshit smooths over the rough edges. But when they care— when they feel deeply about something—they keep their fucking mouths shut."

Oh god. This was worse than I'd thought. "I'm sure you—"

"Thirteen years, I've known the man, and he never said a fucking word about you, so whatever you did to him must have been pretty bad." He stood from the table, chair scraping across the floor, and downed his cup of tea like it was water. Like the heat didn't bother him a bit. "Thanks for the tea. I think I'll head out with Rex to keep an eye on the woods for a bit."

"Yeah, okay," I whispered, my chest tight and my hands shaking. I wanted to breathe, to escape the constant feeling of being hunted by that man, but I couldn't. Not with him in the room. Not with him watching me, waiting for me to fall apart.

But as soon as he hit the archway into the hall, I released all the tension from my body and sagged against the counter. A second too soon, it seemed.

"And by the way, Legs?" Gage stared right at me when I looked up, his eyes boring into mine. "That man is my brother in every way that matters. Don't fuck with him. You two make up and get your shit together, awesome. But if that's not your plan, make sure you don't destroy him on your way out of town this time. You may have gotten away with that when it was Alder looking out for him, but you won't with me."

And then he was gone, and I was left with a mug of green tea, a sick feeling in my stomach, and a handful of tears I couldn't hold back.

Chapter Ten

BISHOP

Funerals had always seemed weird to me. I had no interest in looking at a dead body or in being in the same room with one. Miss had felt the same way, it seemed, which was why we sat in a parlor at the Molnar Funeral Home in Rock Falls paying our respects to some flowers, a couple of pictures of the lady herself, and an urn of her ashes.

"I'm so sorry for your loss." Another gray-haired lady shook Anabeth's hand, whispering the same six words almost everyone in the room had said over the last hour. Anabeth simply smiled that showman's smile and said thank you, probably not knowing who half these people were. Hell, I wasn't sure I knew who they all were.

"What's doing, boss?" Gage plopped into the chair beside me, for once, sans Rex.

"No dog tonight? I'm shocked."

"Dogs don't belong in funeral homes."

"Dogs don't belong in half the places you take Rex. What makes this different?"

"It's a funeral, jackass. I understand social conventions and norms, even if I usually choose to say fuck you to them. Not for something like this, though."

Huh. I never would have thought the man had limits.

He wasn't done, though. "Besides, Molnar's granddaughters are here. They're upstairs playing with Rex."

And suddenly, all was right with the world as I knew it in regards to Gage Shepherd. "That makes a fuckton more sense than your social conventions speech."

"Probably." He settled deeper into his seat, slouching, looking far meaner and more antisocial than even I knew him to be. "You're wearing those shit shoes again."

My dress shoes. "It's a funeral."

He kicked out his leg, showing me the black, lug-soled boots on his feet. "They go with everything. Even those dress pants you like to wear."

"Are we really talking fashion right now?"

"It's function. Those Soul Suckers show up in the middle of this thing, and you're going to be wishing for your boots."

I couldn't really argue with him.

I also couldn't pay him much attention. My eyes sought out Anabeth, my ears trained on the cadence and tone of the words I couldn't quite hear. Gage needed to be second place tonight. I had a redhead with a grieving heart to take care of, even though I had no idea what to do for her. I mean, I knew what I *wanted* to do. Same thing I'd wanted to do since she'd kissed me goodnight at her bedroom door the night before. Since she'd slicked that little pink tongue into my mouth and made me rock fucking hard for her.

None of those options were possible or appropriate for a funeral, though.

Unless she asked.

Fuck, if she asked me to touch her? To taste her and hold her and slide in between those long, sexy legs of hers? I'd probably blow my load like a chump. Like a teenager. Like a man who hadn't been with the woman he loved for fourteen long years.

As I focused on Anabeth and the way her dress hugged every inch of her curves, Gage stiffened beside me, his attention caught by something or someone. I turned, following his sightline. Katie Baker—recently moved back to town and owner of the only restaurant in Justice—worked her way through the throng of people toward Anabeth, while Gage followed her every move. When she stood in front of us, the two women hugged, their whispered conversation too quiet for even me to hear. Meanwhile, Gage kept watching—a little more surreptitiously now that Katie stood less than five feet away. I kept my eyes on Anabeth.

As if she could sense me watching, Anabeth turned just a little, catching me looking at her. Staring, really. Devouring her with my eyes. Her smile changed—went from her act to real. From plastic and fake to the one she only gave a handful of people in her life. Me included. Even tired, pale, and sad, the woman was too beautiful to look away from when she smiled that way. And she was looking at me, making me feel like a fucking king. Like the luckiest man alive to be graced with such a beautiful vision.

"How bad was it?" Gage asked, his voice low and soft. He didn't look my way, though. Instead, his eyes stayed locked on the two women in front of us. On Anabeth and Katie.

I didn't need to ask what he meant. "The worst you can possibly imagine? Multiply it by ten."

He grunted, as if he understood. As if he knew exactly what I meant. And maybe he did. I might never have told him about Anabeth, but he'd seen me that first year after she'd left me. He'd watched me dive into my SEAL training with an energy fueled by something close to rage. I'd hated myself then—hated that I'd somehow lost her, that I'd fucked up bad enough to have her walk away from us. The next year? I'd hated *her*. And it had taken me a long fucking time to stop.

Gage had seen it all, which was why his next question didn't surprise me in the least. "You sure you're willing to risk it again?"

I stared at Anabeth, at the curve of her hip in the dress she wore, at the fancy updo thing she'd done to her hair, at the long line of her neck and the sharp line of her collarbone. I stared at the only woman I'd ever loved, the one who still held a piece of my heart. The one I would give anything to have back in my life and my bed.

My answer was an easy one. "Absofuckinglutely."

Gage took a deep breath and crossed his arms over his chest. "Okay, then."

"What's that mean?"

"Nothing. I just wanted to make sure you knew what you were getting into."

I didn't really have an answer for him. Did I know? Sure—but the last time had ended in a way that had broken my heart and sent my life down a path I hadn't planned for it to go. This time? If Anabeth left me again? I had no idea what I'd do.

But as Katie walked away, Anabeth turned and gave me another soft, tired smile. A real one, not the stage smile she'd been tossing out to every person who approached her. And that look, that raise of her lips I knew was just for me, made every possibility laid out before me worth the risk.

"I do know," I said, smacking Gage on the shoulder as I rose to my feet. "And I'm still all in. You might want to think about diving in yourself at some point."

"And you might want to think about changing your shoes."

A funeral was not the place to flip someone off, so I ignored that comment. For the moment.

Anabeth's smile grew as I crossed the aisle to stand at her side, my left hand on her lower back and my right reaching to shake hands with the people who'd come to pay their respects. And when she sank into me, when her body relaxed and she leaned her shoulder against my chest as if seeking comfort, I stood a little straighter, a little firmer. I shifted into a parade rest sort of stance to support her.

To be the one person she could count on no matter what.

"Thank you," she whispered in between mourners.

"You never have to thank me for caring, Firefly."

"You smell like spearmint."

"Gum. Do you want some?"

"No thanks, but I like the smell on you." Her head landed on my shoulder, just for a second, before the next older gray-haired lady approached.

"I'm so sorry for your loss."

And so the night went. But every time someone new expressed their condolences, every time I had to hear about Anabeth's loss, my resolve firmed up. Fuck loss. I wouldn't be losing Anabeth again.

Chapter Eleven

ANABETH

Katie was going to owe me big.

"More dangly snowflake things. They make the room look festive." The pint-sized brunette had her hands on her hips, accentuating the swell of them with each hop and sway as she practically danced around the dining room at The Baker's Cottage. Every male gaze in the room followed her movements, but she didn't notice. Too worried about making sure each detail was *just so* before the grand opening celebration that evening.

No wonder she hadn't been dating.

And me? I was trying my damnedest not to think about Bishop and dating at the same time. He'd been so sweet at the funeral, so kind and supportive. We'd stood there like a couple, greeting people and accepting the condolences of the mourners. Some of the ones who knew our past, who remembered the younger Bishop and Anabeth, gave us heartfelt smiles. There had been no hate or judgment thrown my way for leaving the way I had all those years ago. Just acceptance, respect for Miss, and a warm, solid hand on my back offering me the support I'd needed. The entire night had been...amazing.

But Gage's words from the other night refused to stop repeating in my head. They'd left me raw and unprotected, flaying my skin wide and exposing feelings I wasn't ready to deal with. Sadly, the man in question—every thick, bearded inch of him—was our babysitter for the day, which meant I couldn't escape his overbearing presence.

"Careful," Shye said quietly as she sidled up beside me. "You've caught the attention of the shark."

"What's the shark?"

"Gage. He keeps staring this way."

I glanced behind me, catching his eyes before looking back to the table of festive plasticware before me. Shye was right; he *was* watching, though she'd been wrong about the staring part. He wasn't just staring—he glared. And deep down, I knew I deserved every hard look he could send me. I deserved so much more.

But I wasn't about to tell a virtual stranger that. "You call Gage the shark?"

She shrugged. "It's the eyes. Eyes that dark are sharklike, you know?"

I did. I totally knew. And he'd made me feel like prey enough to agree with the shark comparison.

As Shye and I counted out forks and spoons, Finn appeared from the back of the restaurant carrying a big, heavy-looking box. "Where do you want this, Katie?"

"Oh, perfect. Anabeth, come here."

Not what I wanted to do—my mixed-up feelings about the younger Kennard brother were still too rough and out of control for me to swallow down—but I pasted on a smile and headed their way. "What's up, boss?"

"These are some of the old tin signs from when this place was a diner forty years ago. There are boxes of them in the basement. Aren't they fun?"

She held up a couple, grinning from ear to ear. Heavy, dirty slabs of metal with chipped paint and advertising for products long gone. Not at all the style of her restaurant.

But Katie didn't seem to notice my hesitation. "See, this is for that chocolate milk stuff everyone used to drink. Oh, and a soda fountain sign. I don't have a soda fountain, but I could put the sign out, right? Remind the customers of what once was so they can see the upgrade. Almost...an homage to Justice's past."

I tried to be excited for her find, but I needed this conversation to end. Finn kept looking at me, watching me with those eyes that were so close to Bishop's unusual gray shade—just a bit bluer. But unlike when Bishop caught my gaze, I didn't feel warm or wanted. Finn's stare left me cold and uncomfortable, and I had a sudden need to disappear.

"Oh, Camden is here," Katie said, smiling toward the door where, indeed, Camden had just walked through. "I needed to ask him something. What was it? Oh, hell. Camden, what were we talking about the other day?"

And then she swept away in a whirlwind of nervous energy and deadline-driven mania.

"Is it just me, or does talking with her make you want to take a nap?" Finn stepped beside me, bumping my shoulder with his. "You ready to put on a show tonight, rock star?"

"I'm far from a rock star, but yes. I'm ready. Tarot is easy." Unless Camden was the one pulling cards, then not so much. But I wasn't about to tell anyone what I'd read for him. "You ready for guard duty?"

He nodded in the most exaggerated fashion as he said, "No. Not at all."

His smile made mine break out, and I reached to smack his arm. Just as my hand made contact, I caught Gage watching us, his face pulled tight into a frown. I took a step away from Finn.

Luckily, Bishop walked in before Finn noticed my retreat, stealing my attention and calming the storm inside of me. He practically stole my breath, he looked so handsome. And I... Well, I was gone for that man all over again. So far gone.

"Hey," Bishop said when he stopped in front of me. His hair looked darker than usual, the persistent rain soaking him, and his eyes seemed even grayer as they focused solely on me.

"Hey yourself."

He glanced around, his brow furrowing when he noticed the streamers all across the ceiling. The ones hitting him in the head. "Well, these are a little low."

"I doubt Katie or Shye, each of whom barely come up to your chest, thought about you tall people."

"Apparently not. Hey, man," he said, directing his attention to Gage who'd walked over. "Deacon called. He needs help bringing over the liquor. Asked if you could drive out to The Jury Room with Finn."

Gage shot me a hard look before returning that dead gaze to Bishop. "Whatever he needs."

"Thanks. And hey, Finn—I didn't see you there. How are you, brother?"

Finn couldn't seem to look Bishop in the eye. "Good. Fine. So, Deacon needs me?"

"Yeah. If you don't mind. I can run over if there's a problem—"

"Nah, he's my boss. I can handle this." Finn disappeared out the front door, dragging Gage—and therefore Rex—along with him. Leaving me alone with Bishop. Or as alone as we could be considering all the people bussing about.

"So, yeah," Bishop said, his smile growing warmer. Deeper. So much more handsome. "Hey."

I grabbed his hand, unable not to touch. "Hey. So... Who's Deacon?"

Bishop wrapped an arm around my waist, pulling my body against his and making my heart flutter. "Alder's best friend and the owner of the old bar and motel at the county line. He calls it The Jury Room."

"Finn works in a bar? Isn't that..."

"Tempting fate? Don't know. He wasn't an alcoholic, and Deacon keeps an eye on him for us, so we try to stay positive about it."

I hummed, inching closer. Licking my lips as his hand dropped lower. His fingers brushing the top of my ass. "What about Elijah? What's he doing these days?"

"Defense attorney out in Denver. Shares his house with Lainie, who's there to get her MBA."

"Wow." That was all I could say. None of that fit with their personalities from when they were younger. Finn had been driven and eager, while Elijah had been a slacker and a jokester. Lainie had simply been a little girl with pigtails and dolls. They'd all changed so much over the last fourteen years.

And I'd missed all of it.

Bishop was still Bishop, though. Still too handsome for his own good. Still looking at me as if I were the only woman in the room. Still such a magnet for me and my heart.

"Excuse me," Shye said as she appeared beside us. "Katie wants more boxes of signs brought up from the basement, and Finn left. Do you think you can grab them for her?"

Bishop didn't let me go, even when I tried to pull away. "Sure. What kind of signs are they?"

I was not a woman who let an opportunity pass me by.

"I can show you." I led him by the hand to the basement stairs off the kitchen, my body humming the entire way. He followed closely, almost too close. Near enough to brush his hand against my hip with every step. I'd only wanted a moment alone with him, a few seconds to say more than hey, but something about this trip to the basement felt electrified. Felt prophetic in a way. The tension grew with each stair down, dragging us like gravity. Like we were meant to be in that cold, dark space.

Just us.

When we reached the bottom of the stairs, I paused. Looking around as my heart slammed a staccato beat in my chest. The basement sat shadowy and quiet, seemingly cut off from the rest of the world. Completely swallowing Bishop and me. We were alone. And so damn close to each other.

"So." Bishop crowded me. Brushing my body with his. "Where are these signs?"

So close. Always so close. The man seduced me with his proximity.

"I'm not sure. I just know what they look like. We might have to hunt a bit."

Bishop hummed, running his hand over the curve of my hip before holding out an arm for me to go ahead of him. I took a deep breath and headed deeper into the dark. The shadows seemed to move, though, and I paid far too much attention to the man following me to notice silly things like pipes running across the floor. At least, until I tripped over one.

Before I could fall, Bishop grabbed my arm and swung me up against his chest. Hard muscles pressed against me, and his rough hands held on to my biceps in a grip just shy of too much. I really wanted too much, though. I wanted him to be strong with me. To overpower me in some way.

I shivered, making Bishop smile in that charming fucker way of his.

"You know what I was thinking about all day, Firefly?"

Oh god, he'd pulled out the big guns with that nickname again. "No, what?"

"Kissing you the other night." He leaned closer, his lips a breath away from mine. "I hope you're not mad about that."

Breathe, Anabeth. Fucking breathe.

"No. I'm not mad." I pulled him closer, rising on the balls of my feet to close the distance between us. "I'm not sorry either."

The look in his eyes, the hunger there. It set my body on fire.

"This is more than nothing," he said, his breath whispering over my face. His lips too close to mine to resist.

"It is. It always has been."

"You sure that's what you want?"

I couldn't lie. Not with him so close. Not with the tension so thick.

"I just want you."

"Thank fuck." He dropped down and stole a kiss, slipping his tongue past my lips when I opened for him.

The kiss started all sweet and easy, calm brushes and gentle pressure. But then I moaned into his mouth—a soft, needful sound —and Bishop broke. His lips grew stronger, his tongue demanding more. Hands tugging, moving us so he could press me against a wall, he kissed me like a man starving to be kissed. Like a man who *needed* to taste me. I kissed him back just as vigorously. Just as needy. And my god, had I missed kissing him. The two times before had been good—surprising, but good. This was better. Hotter.

His touch hard and strong, Bishop caressed every inch he could reach. Kneading his way over my hips and down my thighs, blatantly teasing me through the fabric of my skirt. Cupping my most delicate flesh as he pulled away to whisper a harsh, "Tell me I can touch you, Anabeth."

I nodded, needing the same thing he did. Giving him permission to take it. Bishop didn't hold back, yanking up my skirt and sliding his hand into my panties, finding my clit with a precision that left me gasping. But he didn't stop there. Mouth on mine, tongue stroking inside, he mimicked the movements down below. Brushing, teasing, pressing, rubbing until I had to break the kiss. Had to catch my breath.

And then he started talking.

"Fuck, baby. You're soaked for me. Can't wait to taste you again. Going to eat you for days when I finally get between your legs." He flicked his finger against my clit, making me gasp at the sensation.

"Bishop."

"Let me make you come, Firefly. Let me feel it."

My knees nearly buckled, my panties growing wetter with every second. How could I say no? How could anyone expect me to?

I didn't. Instead, I spread my legs a little wider and grabbed his hand, weaving our fingers together and pushing them inside myself. Pressing him deeper as I retreated. Whimpering my need as he stretched me so damn wide.

"So hot. Always so fucking hot." He leaned closer, sinking his teeth into my collarbone as I pulled my hand completely away from his. I didn't need to help him—he knew how to get me off. He always had. Long before I even knew how to do it myself.

"More, please," I keened, trying to rock my hips, to gain more friction. But he held me in place, keeping me at his will. And I let him. Surrounded by him, weighted down by him, possessed by him...I let it all happen because I wanted him. Always had and always would.

"I've got you, baby," he said, his voice so deep and growly. "I'll treat this pussy so good. I'll make every second so sweet for you. Just stay with me here. Stay with me."

I broke. The words, the double meaning I heard in them, the way his fingers plunged deep inside me and his palm worked my clit. There was no way to resist. The dam holding back my lust and desire and memory of all the things I hadn't allowed myself to think about for years finally burst as I came, as I gripped his shoulders and curled my body into his. As he whispered such filthy sweet endearments in my ear.

"Such a good girl. Just as beautiful as I remember. Feel so good on my fingers. So fucking soft and wet for me." And then he went in for the kill. "I missed you, Firefly. So fucking much."

My heart practically poured right out of my chest even as my body melted against him. "I know you won't believe me, but I missed you too. Every day."

And I had. There was no denying it, no need to hide my weakness. I'd loved this man almost since I had met him. I still did. I probably always would.

Bishop sighed loud and deep, pressing his hips against me as if seeking some sort of relief, some way to bring attention to the hard cock wedged between us. But before I could do anything more for him, he withdrew his hand from between my legs, leaning back just enough to stare down at me. To lock me into place with his gaze. Those gray eyes as dark and demanding as ever. I hadn't seen eyes like his before I met him, hadn't since either. I knew I never would again when he walked away from me.

Not if. *When.* A thought that terrified me. As did the way his eyes went from heated and needy to questioning. Determined.

I wasn't ready for determined Bishop.

"I need to know what happened." When I tried to shake him off, he pressed harder against me, pinning me to the wall. Trapping me there. "I deserve that much. You left, and when I came to find you,

you were already with some other guy. What the fuck did I do that was so bad—"

"Stop." I shook my head, bringing my finger to his lips to quiet him. Unable to hear the pain and anguish in his voice without wanting to cry. "You did nothing wrong."

"Then why were you with someone else?"

Something in his voice, in the look on his face, tore through my battlements. Opening up the place where I stored my secrets and giving me just enough room to tell him that story. To soothe him with one truth. "The man? The one I lived with in Vegas? I wasn't with him like that. Miss sent me to him because I needed to get away from here. He was a friend of hers and nothing more than my roommate for a couple of years while I got my GED and went to vocational school."

Bishop shook his head, looking so confused. "Why didn't you say anything? When I came to find you, why didn't you tell me that? You had to know what I thought when he answered the door."

I had. And I'd fed into it instead of calming him because I'd needed that moment to be the end of us. Something I'd never admitted. Something he needed to understand. "It was easier to get you to leave if you thought I'd moved on."

He jerked back, leaving me cold and empty against the wall. Alone, like always. I curled into myself, tears building in my eyes as I watched him retreat from me.

"I want the whole story, Anabeth." Bishop began to pace, his steps long and loud. Stomping almost. "I deserve that much. You never gave me a fucking reason why you left."

And I never would because to admit what I'd done would break him. Break us forever. A sob ripped through my chest, racking my body hard. "I can't. You'll..."

"I'll what?" Bishop lunged and grabbed my arms, holding me up, staring down at me in a way he never would again if he knew. If I told him. With care and compassion and feelings so strong, I could almost believe he'd forgive me. But he wouldn't. I couldn't even forgive myself. "Tell me, Anabeth. What is it you think I'll do if I know?"

"You'll hate me," I snapped. "You'll never see me the same way, and I can't. I just..."

Bishop stood solid and firm, waiting for me to finish my sentence. Watching as if hoping I would keep talking, but I was done. Out of words. Battlements restored.

Hating myself, knowing he wouldn't stop pushing me unless I made him, I said the only thing I could think of to end the conversation. "Katie's waiting on the boxes."

Bishop reeled as if I'd slapped him with my words. I didn't back down, staring right back at him as he gaped at me. As his own walls came crashing down, his face going from hurt to pissed in two seconds flat.

"You ruined us, Anabeth," he said, his voice empty and lifeless. "Whatever happened—whatever you're keeping from me—it destroyed us both. Don't you get that? I should know what took you away from me. I should know why my heart's been broken for fourteen goddamn years."

But the words wouldn't come. I'd promised myself I wouldn't ever tell him, wouldn't ever bring that pain to his door. A broken heart was nothing in comparison, so I simply shook my head and pressed my lips together as the tears flowed. As I collapsed under the grief and self-hatred that I carried every day. As I watched him shut down.

He grabbed a box of signs and headed for the stairs, leaving me behind.

Alone.

Always.

Chapter Twelve

BISHOP

There was something completely sadistic about sitting in that restaurant and watching Anabeth work the crowd after what happened between us in the basement. Sadistic and cruel, to be honest. Yet, I couldn't leave. Couldn't trade guard positions with one of the men working the party. I couldn't fucking leave her, and that ate at me more than anything else.

So I sat, my cock hard and my mood foul. I watched as she read tarot cards for people and laughed with old friends of both of ours. And I hated myself a little bit more for opening my heart to the fiery redhead fate had once again thrown at me.

"You look ready to kill someone," Finn said as he took a seat on the stool next to mine. He sat like I did—back to the counter, legs spread. Ready to hop up if needed. Ready to fight. He may not have been in the military, but he'd picked up our quirks easily enough.

I shrugged and took a sip of my beer, not taking my eyes off Anabeth. "Just doing my job."

"Guard dog Bishop? Is that what you're saying?"

Fitting. "Woof."

Finn watched the crowd for a long moment, fidgeting. Obviously uncomfortable, though why, I had no idea. At least, not until he opened his mouth.

"I've always felt responsible for Anabeth le—"

"No." I slammed my beer down, drawing attention from a couple at the closest table. Not that I gave a shit. "I get that you two were friends or are friends or had some sort of friend thing going on, I do. And I always respected that. But I don't want you in the middle of my shit, and I certainly don't want to hear a goddamned word of your opinion on why she left."

Finn just nodded, his lips pulled into a flat line. "Understood. Not my story to tell anyway."

We went back to an uncomfortable silence, watching the room again. The rage inside me built with every smile Anabeth gave someone else, every laugh she released that wasn't directed at me. Entertaining the crowd. Sick, jealous bastard described me well at that moment, but I couldn't stop myself from feeling so mean. So angry. So motherfucking sick of the leash she'd had on me since the day we met.

Gage appeared in front of me, blocking my view and only pissing me off more. Not that he appeared to give a single fuck.

"What's wrong with Finn?"

I glanced over, just then noticing how Finn had left the bar. He stood in the corner, watching Anabeth and looking...guilty? But I couldn't care at that moment, didn't have it in me to worry about my little brother, along with the girl who'd ripped my heart out with a spoon and a showman's smile.

"No clue." Rex bumped into my legs, tongue out and tail wagging. "Don't you know dogs shouldn't be in restaurants?"

Gage took the seat beside me, leaning down to pat the mutt's head. "If you think the health inspector is our biggest worry tonight, you're not paying attention."

And I wasn't—not to the possibility of the Soul Suckers coming to town, at least. My focus stayed on Anabeth, too drawn to her not to look. I'd always said the woman was impossible to miss, impossible to ignore, and she proved it to every fucker in that room. I wanted to hate her for it, for beaming and laughing and being social while I seethed, but I couldn't hate her. Not when my heart beat faster every time she even glanced my way, my cock hardening with every flip of her hair. And that just soured my mood even more.

Everything was going about as well as could be expected until the door opened, the pealing of the bell bringing everyone's attention to it. A big, burly man came strolling in with another guy right behind him. Both wearing Soul Suckers vests. They blocked the door, looking intimidating as fuck in their jeans and heavy boots. Intimidating to all the people sitting at the tables, at least. Me? I was ready for them. Let them try to start shit—I was pissed enough to rip them apart with my bare hands. And that bullshit *block the door to scare everyone in the place* move wasn't about to fool me. I wasn't some fucking rookie, and neither were any of the men on my crew.

The two Soul Suckers had just made a huge mistake by walking into Katie's place.

"At least, you've got your boots on tonight." Gage stood and slipped through the crowd to block the kitchen door with Rex beside him. He'd pulled Shye's protection detail for the night, which meant she had to be back there. Good—the last thing we needed was for these fuckers to see her. I had no doubt that's why they'd shown up. Shye's stepbrother was one of their enforcers, and he had some fucked-up notion that the girl owed a debt to the club. Payment for her meant rape or a beating, and there was no way Alder would allow that. Hell, there was no way any of us would. These fuckers weren't getting near her.

And yeah, I was real fucking thankful I had my boots on.

As the two meatheads stood and did their best to look scary, I scanned the room, checking on everyone else. Looking for weak spots. Katie stood on the far side of the bar, a surprised and nervous expression on her face, but Deacon had his hand on her arm. Holding her in place. There were enough men at the tables to keep the rest of the women safe as well. The town always had been a bit of a sausage fest, and that would work in our favor tonight. The only glaring crack in our armor was Anabeth herself, who stood directly in front of our new friends. I hated that she was closer to them than to me, right in the path of whatever danger was about to come our way. She didn't seem to notice, though, or she was used to dealing with a darker sort of crowd. The woman stood unafraid, gorgeous, and looking like a goddamned cherry on a sundae for those fuckers —one they definitely took notice of. The smaller of the two even licked his fucking lips as he stared at her.

I was going to have to kill someone in a minute.

"Looks like quite the party," the big guy in front said, scanning the crowd. "I don't see my friends, though. Maybe someone can help me with that. See, a few weeks back, we sent a couple of guys into town to check in on another friend of ours, and they didn't come back. We've come to find out why."

I rose to my feet, stepping closer, locking eyes with him. He grinned my way. Fucker thought he was the alpha in the room—it would be so much fun to prove him wrong.

"You wasted a trip," I said. "As you can see, your friends aren't here. There's a lost and found at the truck stop over by the county line, though. Little box right by the registers. Maybe you should check there. See if somebody turned them in."

His gaze went hard, his jaw clenching. He changed his

expression quick, though. Smiling again in that arrogant, sarcastic way that meant he thought he had pulled something over on us.

"Or maybe I should start asking around." He flicked a glance at Anabeth, making my heart skip a beat. "There are an awful lot of pretty ladies in this group, and I can be pretty damn persuasive when I need to be."

The fuck he could. I caught Anabeth's eye, nodding toward the back of the restaurant. I wanted her safe and away from them, tucked behind Deacon or Finn or Gage, but she raised her chin and brought out that heart-stopping grin. The showman in her stepping back on stage.

God, I both loved and hated the entertainer side of her.

"I'm reading tarot cards for people tonight," she said, walking closer to the guy, swinging her hips and giving me a motherfucking heart attack. "Why don't you pull a card so we can see what they say? Maybe they'll show you a path to your friends."

"You got a witch in this town?" He looked her up and down, eyeing every curve like a dog salivating over a steak. "Okay, witchy woman, do your best."

Anabeth gave him a flirty sort of grin and held up her deck of cards, the fan of them resting on her fingertips. But something wasn't right. I knew her deck, had seen her with it a million times. That wasn't her deck.

That was one Miss had used. One she'd refused to let me touch. One she'd joked should only ever be handled by the Hansen women.

If I remembered right, Anabeth had just pulled the deck that hated men.

Okay, so this might be fun.

"Pick one"—Anabeth's smile grew—"and I'll tell you your future."

He huffed a laugh but did as she suggested, pulling a single card from the deck and looking it over. "A man with a hoe...fitting for tonight, don't you think?" He laughed with his friend, the two eyeing Anabeth even harder. "So what's it mean, witch?"

Anabeth took the card back, pursing her lips in a concerned expression. "Oh dear, the Seven of Pentacles. That's probably not the best card to read for you. Maybe pick another one."

"Fuck that. Tell me what my card means."

Anabeth shot a glance my way and winked. Motherfucking winked. She was going to get herself killed, and I was still farther away from her than the man at the door.

"The Seven of Pentacles represents the promise of success..." She paused as the guy smiled, and then she went in for the kill. "...unfulfilled. The rosebuds never grow, and the farmer is defeated by mother nature herself. The card is about loss and deception, crushing failure and disappointment. This card calls you out as a loser."

The guy opened his mouth twice without speaking, looking shocked. Looking pissed. His hesitation gave me just enough time to reach Anabeth. To move in beside her as the guy found his words.

"You fucking cunt."

Primitive, but if the way Anabeth stiffened was any indication, effective. I slid in front of her as the guy's face turned red, as he took a single step toward her, looking ready to kill.

Time to play. "You don't want to do that."

He practically snarled, looking from Anabeth to me and back before zeroing in on me. "Where the fuck are our brothers? We know you did something to them."

"Don't know what you're talking about, but like I said—the truck stop at the county line has a lost and found. You should really head there. Now."

The room, already tense and silent, went deathly still as the kitchen door swooshed open and closed again. I didn't need to turn to know what I'd see—Alder had just walked in. And if I had to guess, he was looking big, mean, and absolutely ready to kill a fucker. Game on.

"We got a problem here?" He strolled up all casual-like, his arms folded over his chest and a hard stare on his face. "I don't remember seeing Tweedledee and Tweedledum on the guest list."

"Ah, the illustrious Alder Kennard." The Soul Sucker clapped three times as if giving my brother a standing ovation. "I hear you're good at what you do, which seems to be keeping us from getting what's ours. But hey, I'm a reasonable man. I can barter. You burned down our kitchen, and I think you owe us a little something. Since we can't find our brothers, the least we can do is bring back the bitch who owes us money." The dumbfuck took a step closer to my brother, glaring...up at him. A man wasn't so intimidating when he was six inches shorter than you, I'd guess. Still, the guy tried. He probably even got under Alder's skin when he spat out an angry, "Where's Pistol's whore?"

Alder held his temper, though his jaw ticked and clenched. Those words definitely pissed him off. "Ain't got any whores around these parts. I think you should head on out of town if that's the sort kind of thing you're looking for."

Dumb and Dumber focused completely on Alder, looking ready to fight. Not paying any attention to the rest of the room. I took advantage of their distraction to back Anabeth toward the kitchen. She resisted at first, her hands on my shoulders and her steps slow as she watched my brother verbally spar with the Soul Suckers. It wasn't until I grabbed Katie's arm from Deacon that Anabeth finally, quietly, surrendered and went with the flow. Gage opened the kitchen door and directed both women through it, following behind them. Their guard on duty. I caught Anabeth's concerned gaze as she was herded toward the back exit, but I didn't say anything. I couldn't. I needed her gone—needed her safely tucked away where these fuckers couldn't get their hands on her—so I could fight beside my brother.

Once Gage shut the door behind him, I headed back up front to do just that. I reached the standoff at the front door in time to hear big, dumb, and mean say, "He *will* get the little bitch. It's only a matter of time."

Alder looked ready to tear the guy's head off with his bare hands at that point. "You tell Pistol if he even thinks of coming near *my* girl, he'll have to deal with me. And I'm not afraid to bury a body or ten."

"You're making a mistake."

Alder smiled, a predatory look on his face. "Son, the only mistake here is you being in Justice. You've got two minutes to be on the road before we pull out the explosives and turn your unavoidable retreat into a game of *Frogger*."

The guy looked around the restaurant, probably just noticing that almost all the women had been quietly escorted out of the dining area. He stood in a room filled with loggers—tall, brawny men who weren't afraid to get their hands dirty. No matter what that meant. I saw the moment he accepted defeat, caught the flash of fear when he realized how we outnumbered him. Didn't stop him from opening his stupid fucking mouth when he caught me watching him, though.

"Tell that firecrotch witch of yours she'll be seeing me soon."

It took me real effort not to slam my fist into his face. "I don't fucking think so."

The guy grinned, looking way too cocky for my liking, before turning and heading out into the night. Alder stood stock-still, watching. Waiting.

I hated waiting. "Think it was a good idea to let them walk?"

"We had a roomful of witnesses." A fire filled his eyes when he looked my way, one burning hot with frustration. "I doubt anyone would have talked if we'd taken them out, but I couldn't risk it. The last thing Shye needs is me in jail, even for one night."

I could understand that logic. I didn't like it, but I got it. Without Alder to keep her safe, Shye was easy pickings. Even with the rest of us watching over her. In Alder's mind, no one could keep her as safe as he could. I understood that too, because while I trusted my brothers to keep an eye on Anabeth, I knew my level of protection would go a step further.

Because I loved her.

Always had.

Always would.

When the roar of motorcycle engines broke the silence, Alder barked, "Deacon."

The man in question appeared from the bar area with Finn at his side. "On it."

The two disappeared outside, probably to follow the bikers out of town. Making sure they didn't set up an ambush somewhere. Alder glared out the door one last time before heading for the kitchen. For Shye.

I followed him, needing to see Anabeth. Wanting to make sure she was safe. Only then would the tightness in my chest disappear. Or so I hoped.

When Alder pushed through the swinging door, he headed straight for his woman, picking her right up off the floor and holding her tight as he whispered in her ear. So open about his affection for her, so protective. And she obviously felt the same because she clung to him, completely oblivious to anything *but* him.

And like Alder with Shye, I sought out Anabeth, unable not to. Pale but with her chin up, she stood at the back of the kitchen with her arms wrapped tight around her middle. Scared but defiant. I wanted to go to her, to grab her and wrap myself around those curves. To soothe the fear inside of her and promise to take care of her. To keep her safe. I wanted to make her mine and vow to always protect her.

And I would. Fuck the past, fuck the story, fuck all of it. Life was too short not to jump in with both feet. And for her, I would. Just not in a fucking restaurant kitchen.

Chapter Thirteen

ANABETH

He wasn't going to come to me.

I knew it, saw it on his face and in his hard stance. Bishop wanted to comfort me but wouldn't allow himself that, and I deserved his distance. I could deal with my own adrenaline crash, though. I'd been dealing with fear and pain and heartbreak for a long time all by myself. Tonight was no different.

Well, the lust I felt in regards to seeing Bishop be so brave... That was new. He'd looked ready to kill, and for some crazy reason, I'd liked that. A lot. Too much.

With a sigh, Alder put Shye back on her own feet, though he kept her tucked into his side. He looked positively lethal in that moment as he towered over her. Her protector ready to knock everyone out of their way. "I'm taking her home."

"Be careful out there," Bishop said. He bumped fists with his brother and leaned in close to whisper to the little blonde. I couldn't hear what he had to say. She smiled, though, so it had to be something good.

When he rose to his full height once more, his eyes immediately zeroed in on mine, and this time, he looked pure predator. On the hunt and hungry, and I was his prey. My knees shook and my heart raced—*that look*. God, he didn't even need to say a word to get me naked when he looked at me like that. He'd never been so bold, so confident. The man was a beast. He didn't need to pick me up like Alder had Shye or soothe me with comforting words. His intentions were perfectly clear on his face.

I would be his tonight, and he wouldn't be sweet about it.

"Let's go." Two words, that was all he gave me, but my breath caught and my hands shook. His intensity was hard enough to bear standing a room apart with others around us—I couldn't imagine what would happen when we ended up alone. This was going to be the longest drive home ever.

I crossed the kitchen, making the move to bring us back together. To put us in the same space. His eyes nearly burned a hole through me as he waited, watching every step with interest. And when I finally reached him, when I stood close enough to smell his cologne, he grabbed my hand. Sparks tingled from that touch, and he branded me with a lustful look before turning and dragging me across the dining room.

Without a single word of goodbye or thanks, I followed Bishop outside and through the rain to his truck. He opened the door for me but didn't move out of the way, forcing me to rub against him as I passed, placing his hand on my ass to help me into the vehicle.

He was trying to kill me.

The rain splattered against the windshield, obscuring my view as he ran around the front and opened his door. Muscles bunched and stretched when he pulled himself inside, and then he was there. Sharing the same space, the same air. Sitting so close and yet miles and miles away. A distance I wanted to cross but couldn't. I could only wait, could only stare.

His hair lay wet against his forehead, his shoulders dark from the water. Hot and wet and so very strong. And mine. Even if only for the night.

He didn't start the engine right away. Instead, he sat quiet and still, breathing hard but not saying anything. Still so close but not touching me. I craved his touch, needed it like I needed air. And still, I waited for him. The overhead light went out, leaving the two of us alone in the darkness. Tension growing, heat building. Nothing but him and me and the sounds of us breathing while the rain fell outside.

When the windshield began to fog up, I gave in to my need and whispered the only word I could. "Bishop."

His name on my lips broke something. Broke the tension and the stillness. Broke him. Bishop grabbed me, yanking me across the bench seat and dragging me into his lap. The feel of him under me, his hands on my body, his roughness—I broke too.

I pushed him, forcing him to angle his body on the seat so I didn't have the steering wheel at my back. So I could rock and thrust and move over him. Because this was what we wanted, what we needed. A reminder of those days before I'd left, when making out in a car was worth the risk of getting caught. When we were too hot for each other to wait until we got someplace more private. And just like back then, I locked my lips over his, groaning when he plunged his tongue into my mouth and wove his fingers into the hair at the back of my neck to tug me closer. To control my depth and speed and movements. So hot, so damn sexy and domineering.

With a growl like some sort of wild animal, Bishop moved under me. Jerking his hips against mine, groaning and panting as he found just the right spot. The one that made me gasp and fall over him. The one that teased my clit through our clothes as I rolled over him.

My wet panties were no match for his jean-covered erection. Even through the layers, I could feel his heat. His need. And I knew mine matched his.

Bishop broke the kiss with a groan that sounded too close to pain. "Do you have any idea how much I wanted to grab you in there? How scared I was that they'd get to you before I could?" His words were like sandpaper, abrading my skin and heart, his voice dark and rough as he said, "You drive me fucking crazy, Anabeth."

He did the same to me, but words were too hard. Too foreign in that moment. I could only feel, could only act. Could only roll my hips against his. We couldn't have sex in the truck right there on Main Street no matter how dark and abandoned it seemed, but a little something—a reminder of our high school days—seemed possible. I hadn't dry humped a man in years, had forgotten how good it felt. How exciting the moment could be when you were in a semi-public place.

I wanted to remember, and thankfully it seemed Bishop did as well.

He grabbed onto my hips as I gripped his shoulders and worked my body over his. Letting my weight do most of the work. Wanting to watch him come apart under me. Needing to see it before I followed him. Before he made me come again. Because he would—I had no doubt about that.

And those words, I could find.

"Please." I bit his lower lip, smiling when he jerked against me. "Let me make you come. Please, Bishop."

He reached between us, unfastening his jeans and opening his fly wide. Two thin layers of cotton were all that stood between us fucking right there in his truck. Parked on the street for anyone to see. I'd never hated underwear more.

"I love it when you beg." He arched and moaned as I soaked the dark fabric covering his cock. "I've dreamed about you begging,

Firefly. All these years, I've thought about you begging me to make you come, to take you back. And here you are fulfilling the first part of that fantasy. Your greedy little pussy can't stay away, can it?"

He tugged me down harder, rolling his hips against me as he thrust and jerked and groaned. As he rocked my body over his and teased me with his hardness. Breathing hard, unable to do anything more than ride him as he bucked, I let the sensations take over my body. Let him lead me right to the edge of pleasure.

And push me over it.

He came with a grunt and a hard hold on me, lifting me up as he arched his back. So strong, so sexy. So male. The sight of him made my own orgasm inevitable. And when I followed him, when I fell over that edge chanting his name, I knew I'd lost any fight I'd had in me. There was no possibility of staying away from him. No way to stop this fall.

Bishop held me for what felt like seconds or what could have been hours. Time had lost all sense of meaning in the wake of such a complete surrender. When we'd caught our breaths, Bishop lifted me off his lap and set me back on the seat, but not before kissing me again. Long, deep kisses that did nothing to quiet my need for him.

"That's it," he said suddenly, reaching into the glove box for a stack of napkins. He handed me two before dealing with his own mess, then he refastened his jeans and started the truck. All while not looking at me. All very...succinct. My stomach twisted, unsure what was happening. Why he'd moved so quickly. What "that's it" meant.

"Bishop—"

"I need to get you home." He pulled out of the spot and turned to head toward Widow's Ridge, giving me nothing more. Driving way too fast for the conditions.

I couldn't deal with the silence. "Shouldn't we talk about this?"

"No."

"Bishop, please—"

"Anabeth, if you say one more word, I'm going to pull this truck over and fuck you on the hood. So if you'd rather I take you to bed where I can lick your pussy without the entire town knowing about it, you'll wait until we get to your place."

Oh lord. I bit my lip and clenched my thighs, holding myself together. I should have told him no, half wanted to say the word just to keep from falling down the rabbit hole again. But I stayed quiet instead, watching him drive. Knowing what was coming as soon as we made it back to the farmhouse. He wouldn't be gentle with me. This wouldn't be like our first time in the woods or all the times after that when we'd been young and dumb and exploring. No, we both knew what we liked now. What we wanted physically in a partner. He wasn't a young man anymore, and his muscles proved it. Bishop wouldn't be gentle—he'd tear me apart and put me back together with his body.

And I could hardly wait.

The drive to the house passed in a heated silence, both of us on edge. Me refusing to say a word for fear he'd go through with the whole pulling over and fucking me on the hood thing. Not that I'd be against it, though the rain would make things uncomfortable for sure.

He flew over the flooded road up to the ridge, not even bothering to slow down at the sight of water flowing over the gravel. Good, because if I had to wait one extra minute for him to touch me again, I might explode.

The second he pulled to a stop in the driveway, I jumped out of the truck and rushed to the porch. Bishop followed, slower, not caring that the rain soaked him, keeping his eyes locked on me. Giving chase. Making my heart leap in my chest at the possibilities of what would happen when he caught me. My keys shook as I unlocked the door, my breaths coming too fast. I wanted inside, wanted to take this man to my bed. Wanted to experience a night in his arms.

On my fourth attempt, the key found the spot, and I finally made it inside. Bishop followed me still, never breaking eye contact as he shut the door and locked it. Safety first, even though he looked ready to pounce.

And then I waited. Breathless and anxious. He didn't make me wait for long.

"Are you wet?" he asked as he kicked off his boots.

I nodded, not caring if he meant from the rain or more. That cocky smile of his kicked up, and he ran a thumb over his bottom lip before tugging his shirt off from behind his neck. "Are you dripping for me, Firefly?"

I might have whimpered. I might even have shivered in response to that question. I definitely nodded, though. His hands went to the front of his jeans, one palm pressing against the hard ridge as his long, rough fingers pulled open the fastenings.

"You've got five seconds to get where you want to be before I throw your ass on the ground and fuck you." He raised an eyebrow when I didn't move, that smile spreading. "One...two—"

I took off at a run, slipping around the corner and heading for the stairs that would take me up to my bedroom. He hit the bottom step as I reached the top landing, his footsteps pounding almost as loud as my heart. Oh god. He was fast. So fast. I wasn't sure if I'd make it. Couldn't tell if there was time to reach the big, soft bed I'd often dreamed of having him in.

I was about five feet from my goal when his strong hands grabbed me around the waist. I squealed as he lifted me off my feet, as he picked me up and tossed me onto the mattress. Wanting to see what was coming for me, I tried to roll over, to face him. But he was bigger than me and stronger. I couldn't break his hold, couldn't roll or buck or throw him off. Not that I really wanted to—I was happy to let him lead, to surrender to what he wanted.

And what he wanted was to hold me down, ruck up my skirt, and shove my panties to the side before plunging his fingers inside me. I hadn't known it, but I'd wanted that too. A lot. Enough that I could feel my arousal dripping down my thighs as he moved behind me.

"You're so fucking wet, baby. You like me taking over, don't you?" He pressed his weight into me as I gasped out a yes, as I shook and fisted the sheets.

As I slammed my body back to fuck his hand. "Yes, yes. More. Bishop, please."

"Gonna take good care of this sweet pussy. Don't you worry about that."

He pulled away and yanked me up by my hips, forcing me to my knees. Putting my ass on display for him. He took advantage too. Running his hands over my curves, sliding them between my thighs and up-up-up. Teasing me. Always teasing me. Until he stopped teasing.

With a slight tug and ripping sound, my panties disappeared, too delicate to last against his desire. I thought for sure he'd drive inside me, was absolutely positive he'd fill me up with one deep, hard thrust. Instead, he grabbed my ass and pulled my cheeks apart, leaning in to lick me from my clit all the way to my asshole.

"Bishop. Fuck." I gasped and shook, hands grabbing at the quilt under me as he attacked with a single-minded focus that had me seeing stars.

"Fucking starving for you," he said, groaning as he used his tongue to punish me. To lick me from one end to the other. To tease my clit until I rocked and jerked against his face.

Endless. His assault seemed endless. Every time I got close enough to come, he'd back off. Hands gripping my hips, shoulders forcing my thighs apart, he took his time. Never pushing too hard. Making me sweat and keen and need, until there were no words to say. No comprehension of time or space or sound. All I knew, all I could focus on, was the deep, angry need that kept trying to swallow me whole. I drowned in it.

And then he made it worse.

He plunged two fingers inside me as he suckled my clit, holding me still when the wave of desire finally crashed around me. Hands on the headboard, I shook and screamed and came all over him, unabashed and completely lost to the moment. And he dragged me through it, refusing to stop. Licking up every drop of my release as he groaned long and rough.

Before the pulses even stopped, Bishop yanked his hand away and thrust inside, hard and thick and so fucking good. He pushed in deep, dragging himself almost all the way out on every pass. Snapping his hips against mine until my body couldn't take another inch. Until the feeling of him inside me pushed me right back off the ledge.

I came again, unable not to. Practically crying as the pleasure broke over me. As he filled me over and over and over again, never slowing down. Never pausing.

"Fucking perfect," he grunted, placing one hand over mine on the headboard to steady us. "Just like I remember. Perfect fucking pussy squeezing my cock. Want to feel you, baby. Want to come deep inside you. Claim this cunt as mine and mine alone."

And he did. He claimed me hard, riding me until I had to brace both hands against the headboard to keep from hitting my head on it. Thrusting, groaning, snapping, and biting at me until I crested one more time, until he pressed deep and came with a grunt that I could practically feel. Until we ended up a tangled heap of messy hair and sweaty skin and half-removed clothing.

Until everything felt perfect, even if just for a moment.

Chapter Fourteen

BISHOP

Motherfucker, I came inside her. I hadn't meant to, had totally thought about grabbing the condom in my wallet to cover myself before sliding inside the heaven of her sweet pussy, but I'd lost my fucking mind at her taste. One lick, and some sort of animalistic need rose within me. I hadn't just fucked her. I'd claimed her. And I wouldn't be letting her go again.

"You're going to have to get up," I said as I stumbled out of bed. "We need a shower after that."

She groaned, looking half dazed and tired. A fact that made my chest swell with something close to pride. I'd done that—fucked her so well she couldn't speak. And I definitely had plans to do it again. Not yet, though.

I leaned over her, trapping her underneath me, grinning when her arms came up around my neck and her body turned into my hold. "Stay for now. I'll come get you in a minute."

She mumbled something that sounded like okay as she fell back to the mattress. Exhausted. Sated.

Fuck yeah.

I headed into the bathroom alone, figuring I could let the water run hot before I brought Anabeth with me. I wanted her pliant and accepting, wanted her just as soft and warm as she had been minutes before. Shoving her under a cold spray of water would ruin the moment. As would making her stand in the chilly bathroom and wait.

Turning the shower taps to hot, I caught a reflection of myself in the mirror. Caught a glimpse of the body I hadn't had when I was a young man. Something made me stop and look, made me rise to my full height and truly see what I tended to overlook every day. Me...the adult version.

Bigger, a little hairier, and definitely more solid than I'd been all those years ago. The muscles had come with age and a fitness routine born from years of SEAL training. With beach workouts and boot camp and hell weeks, the foundation of which stayed with me to this day, driving me to continue to build and strengthen and make sure I ran at top form. But the scars...those had come with missions. With good and bad plans and directions. Those had come with experiences and stories I'd never wanted to share with anyone else. I hadn't really thought about them in years, hadn't catalogued each one and given consideration to the hows and whys and whos behind them. But with the knowledge that Anabeth would see them—the one woman who'd known all of me before I'd earned a single mark on my body— they seemed to almost glow. There was no missing them, no hiding them. No brushing off the past I'd lived or the things I'd done.

This was me. All of me. And she'd have to accept the good with the bad to have me. If she even wanted me.

The woman herself appeared behind me, watching. Those blue

eyes I'd stared into a million times in the past catching mine before sliding over my body the same way my own had. My mouth went dry, and I stood rigid. Oddly worried that I wouldn't pass her inspection. Almost more so that I would.

"This one," she whispered, tracing a long, wide scar that wrapped around the right side of my chest and waist. Thin but deep, the scar looked almost snakelike against my skin.

I grunted, staring at her face. Unable to look away as I laid out my history. "Knife fight in Afghanistan. Guy had planted IEDs along the highway and taken out two Army transport units. We were sent in to remove the threat."

"And did you?"

"I wouldn't be standing here if I didn't." I grabbed her hand, forcing it down to another scar. Smaller, thinner, and right against my hip bone. "As SEALs, we were all supplied with an Ontario Mark 3 knife and taught to use them for survival. We were also trained to be physically fit and to push our bodies to the absolute limits. The IED guy was good with a knife—better than me—but he didn't have my endurance. I lost a fuckton of blood but kept fighting, kept driving into him until the last plunge." I pressed her hand against that little scar. "This was his final try to fight back before he died. He nicked the bone, and it still hurts sometimes when the weather turns extra cold."

She hummed, leaning down to kiss that little scar, not looking disturbed by the story I'd told. Not taking her hands off me either. I breathed a little easier at that. Anabeth took a step to the side, her hands warm and teasing against my shoulders. My cock responded to her touch, to her nearness. I was ready to take her, to pin her to the vanity and fuck her until she broke. Until she came screaming my name again. But she seemed to want this time to look and feel the changes that had come with our separation. So I waited.

Wanting and needy, but patient. I'd always been so fucking patient with this girl.

"This one." She kissed my shoulder with her hand on my arm. With a hold on me that felt tight and real and perfect. I didn't need to see to know which scar she meant.

"Sniper fire."

She stiffened, her nails pinching as she grabbed me tighter. "Aren't snipers usually, like, really accurate?"

I laughed low and rough, remembering. "Yeah. And if it weren't for Gage, the sniper would have been much more accurate. Fucker realized the guy was on the roof just before I did and dove for me."

"Really?"

I nodded. "He's got the matching scar on his opposite shoulder. Bullet went through him and into me."

"That's...a good friend."

Understatement. "He's a brother to me."

She hummed and moved around in front of me, leaning against the counter. "I don't think he likes me much."

"You're a threat."

"To him?"

Not even close. "To me."

Her face went still, her eyes locked on mine. I didn't want to talk about the end, though. Didn't want her to acknowledge the fact that she'd be leaving eventually. Because there was no way I would let her go without a fight. There was also no way she was ready to hear that. So I stayed quiet, waiting her out.

Eventually, she sighed and ran her hands over my shoulders again, watching as her fingers pressed into my flesh. As I flexed under her touch.

"I don't know these parts of you."

I pulled on her hand, bringing her closer so I could wrap my arms around her and lean down to take her earlobe into my mouth.

The one with three silver hoops in it—the one that didn't have any holes the last time I saw her.

"I don't know these parts of you." I ran a finger along the piercing through the cartilage in her ear. "What's this?"

"It's a Daith piercing. Helped relieve my migraines."

"I didn't know you got migraines."

"I didn't. They came up in the last four years or so."

I hummed, thinking about how much we'd both missed. How much we needed to learn and relearn about one another. Once we had the time.

But all that could wait, because I had a naked and willing woman in my arms. And I refused to waste another second.

"C'mon, Firefly." I grabbed her hand and dragged her into the shower behind me, my lips kicking up on one side as I watched her heavy tits jiggle. "I want to get you clean so I can make you dirty again."

Her laugh echoed against the tiles. "Dirty, huh?"

I grabbed her ass and lifted her, loving the way her long legs wrapped around me. Groaning at her wet pussy meeting my abs. "I plan on getting you filthy."

And I did. I fucked her against the tiles first then bent over the vanity just as I'd wanted. Took her on the floor of her room when I couldn't stand to watch that ass sway as she walked to the bed. I buried myself inside her for hours, in every position, using every trick I'd learned to keep her trembling and needy. To please her. And never once did I reach for a condom. Never once did she ask me to either. It was stupid and irresponsible and risky, but I couldn't help myself. I needed her bare and raw, nothing in between us. Nothing in the way.

Because there was a whole lot of shit already keeping us apart.

———

ANABETH

I woke up aching in places that hadn't hurt in years and wrapped in the arms of the one man who'd ever made my heart hurt as well as my body. He slept on without me, looking absolutely delicious. And big. My god, the man had gotten so big.

Quiet and careful, I rolled away from Bishop and out of bed. I needed a moment to myself, a minute to think, and a strong cup of tea to soothe my nerves. Last night had been tremendous, but morning had come. And with that, things would change. They'd have to.

I padded downstairs with the lights off, the early-morning dawn hidden behind that heavy, gray sky. I was tired of rain. I knew the tendencies of the season—that the front would blow past before winter came roaring in—but the memories of late summers spent outside trying to find shelter from the endless water falling from the skies over Justice haunted me. I didn't want those memories—didn't want to think about what we'd done and found out there in the woods. The abandoned logging roads, the ancient hunting stands in the trees. The old barn where my life had almost ended.

Bishop's heavy footfalls pulled me from that thought spiral, forcing me to focus on the man himself. The sexy, sleepy man with the mussed hair and the tired scowl on his handsome face. The one who made my heart come to life in a way no one else could.

He walked into the kitchen shirtless, thick, gray sweat pants hanging low on his hips and that damn V of muscle over his hip bones making me stupid as I stared. No man in real life had that— only celebrities and people paid to work out. Bishop shouldn't have had that, but he did, and I wanted to lick up and down that trail over and over again until he—

"Need coffee."

His grumbled declaration yanked me from my dirty thoughts and had me smiling. "Miss didn't drink coffee."

He shot a glare my way before dragging his eyes to the kettle that had begun to whistle. Looking absolutely miserable. "Caffeine?"

"I always figured you for a morning person in your adulthood." I nodded toward the table and opened a cabinet, pulling out what had to be the least-used appliance in that kitchen. "Miss understood that her guests might like coffee even if she didn't, so she bought herself one of these pod-making things a few years back."

I plugged in the machine and grabbed the directions, unsure how to use the thing. Bishop appeared behind me, all warm and giving me no personal space as he pressed his body against mine and wrapped his arms around me...

To reach the coffee machine.

"I got this," he said before planting a wet kiss against my neck. "Make your tea."

We worked side by side, me pouring water and steeping tea, him pouring water and staring at that machine as if his irritation alone would make the thing brew faster. I held my tongue until he'd taken the first sip, until he moaned much like the way he had last night when I'd taken him in my mouth. A favorite memory for sure.

"Feel better now?"

He hummed and sighed. "Someone kept me up too late last night."

"Oh, really?" I took a step back when he focused those gray eyes on me. "You're going to blame all that on me? As if you didn't want to be woken up with my mouth on you."

He once again shifted into predator mode as he took a single step in my direction. "Oh, I wanted it, all right." He set his cup down and slipped in front of me. Crowding me against the counter. Pressing his hips into my stomach and proving how much he wanted me. "Still want it. Your tea ready?"

The change in conversation threw me, and I had to think about his words before I could answer. "Yeah. Should be."

"Good." He reached for the sugar bowl, the one Miss had always used. The one still filled with cubes instead of granulated sugar. "One or two?"

"Just one."

He dropped a cube in my mug and handed it to me. "Let's sit for a few. I need to finish this coffee to get my brain moving."

Something about his face in that moment, his sweetness at remembering the sugar, it called to me. Weakened my resolve. Weakened my filter.

"I missed you so much." My whispered declaration caught me by surprise, filling me with a sense of dread. We'd already fought over this—we didn't need to revisit it. Luckily enough, he didn't seem to want to either. Instead, he held me tight. Breathing me in as I clutched him to me. As I leaned into his chest, needing to chase the feeling of comfort I received whenever he held me close. Needing to take a moment and appreciate that we were there, together. Again.

Bishop rubbed my back, curling his body around mine as he whispered, "Missed you too. Every day. I didn't pine for you, but..."

"It never stopped hurting."

"No, it didn't." He sighed again, pulling me tighter for a few seconds before letting go. "C'mon, Firefly. Let's sit and enjoy the morning. There's nothing we can do about the past right now."

No, there wasn't. So I followed him to the table, and I simply smiled and took a seat when he yanked two chairs close together so we didn't have to be separated. I drank my tea as he sipped his coffee, both of us unwilling to stop touching, to be apart, to put space between us. And all the while, I fought to keep my hands from shaking. He'd notice that, and he'd ask about it. He'd want to know what had me ready to cry right there at the table.

And I still couldn't tell him. Could never tell him.

He'd missed me, and I'd missed him—every day, he'd said. Every day for the fourteen years we'd been apart. That deep ache had never left me for even a day, and I'd hated it. Hated that I'd messed up so badly. Hated that there would be no coming back from those mistakes. Hated all the years apart and the pain and the lost time together.

Hated that Bishop would never talk to me again once he knew the truth.

And as much as it pained me to think about, as much as it was the last thing I wanted to think about, part of me hated Finn Kennard for his part in destroying us.

Chapter Fifteen

BISHOP

About midmorning—after three cups of coffee and plenty of time spent with me gripping a handful of Anabeth's ass as I fucked her against the kitchen counter—I finally heard from Gage. He'd gotten stuck because of the flooding the night before and hadn't wanted to risk coming up to the house in the dark, but he'd be on his way after a shower. Which meant I had about half an hour to get Anabeth naked again before we were invaded and forced to behave ourselves.

I could do a lot in thirty minutes.

"Gage will be here soon," I said as I walked into her bedroom...

And stopped dead in my tracks.

Anabeth stood against her dresser, wearing nothing but a skimpy pair of lacy pink panties and a questioning expression. "For what?"

But I didn't want to think about Gage at the moment. I didn't want to think at all. That lace—something about it, about the way her skin peeked through the thin fabric, drove me out of my fucking mind.

Thirty minutes wasn't nearly enough time. "You getting started without me?"

She smiled, truly smiled in a way that reached her eyes and made her look so fucking real. Killing me with a look.

"I was about to take a shower. We've gotten a little sweaty since the last one."

I tossed my phone onto the bed and dropped my pants. "Let's go, then."

Saucy little smirk on those cock-sucking lips I loved, she bent at the waist, keeping her eyes on mine as she dragged the slip of lace around her hips down, down, down those long legs she'd had wrapped around my waist not too many hours before. My waist, my chest, my face...good times. And about to get even better.

I chased her into the bathroom, enjoying every laugh she gave, every smile. My girl was happy, and that made my long-dead heart practically sing.

"Why are you looking at me like that?" Anabeth asked as I herded her under the warm spray of water.

"Like what?"

"Like you're about to swallow me whole. You look like you want me in your throat."

This girl. I laughed, unable to hold it in. "That's the way I'm looking at you? Because that wasn't at all what was on my mind."

"Oh. Then maybe that's what was on mine." She shrugged and lowered herself to her knees, looking up at me in a way that made my heart slam in my chest. My god, was she pretty. Those curves, that smile, her kneeling in front of me with her lips so close to my cock and her hands on my thighs? A dream come true.

I didn't get the chance to respond to her, though. Before I could even move the shower spray so she didn't end up cold or drowning, she had me in her mouth. Her hot, wet mouth. Sucking hard. Pulling deep. Making me dizzy with lust and the need to fuck that pretty face.

"Good goddamn." I rocked my hips, unable to hold back as she sucked my cock deep. No teasing, no tentativeness, no slow start—she went all in from the first swallow. I groaned and growled, thrusting gently into that sensational mouth of hers, loving how her pink lips looked stretched around me. "Perfect. Your mouth is so fucking perfect. Made for sucking my cock, isn't it?"

Anabeth groaned, one hand resting on my thigh while the other tugged on my balls. Pushing me to the edge so fast. She enacted an all-out assault on my dick, and I loved every second of it. Not that there were a lot of them. The woman drove me wild, and watching her suck my cock ranked right up there with some sort of fantasy come true. I was ready to blow in an embarrassingly small number of minutes.

"Gonna come, Firefly. Gonna cover you in my come, mark that wicked body as mine." I grunted as I fisted her hair, fucking her harder. Stronger. Faster. Until there was nothing but her, nothing but sensation, nothing but her lips and her tongue and that mouth that was made for sin.

Until I pulled out, shivering and shaking as I groaned her name. As I painted her neck and chest with my come.

"Have mercy." I nearly fell backward, my legs too weak to hold me up, as she ran her tongue over the length of me one last time. "That was fucking amazing, but I'm not as young as I once was."

"No, you're not." She rose to her feet, rubbing her breasts up the length of me, her hand still teasing my cock. "You're even better."

Ah, fuck. My saucy girl. I yanked her against my chest, kissing her deep. Nibbling on her lips and stroking my tongue against hers as I moved us under the spray. Five minutes. If she could just give me five minutes to recover from that mind-blowing orgasm, I'd fuck her good against the shower wall. I'd pin her with my hips and hold her hands above her head so she couldn't move, and then I'd make sure she saw exactly how much better I was.

Okay, if my half-hard cock was any indication, I might only need four minutes.

"You want me to fuck you right here?" I bent down to suck on her nipple as I slipped a hand between her thighs. Soft and wet met my exploring fingers, her thighs spreading to give me room. Wanting and needy, just the way I liked her.

I popped off her tit and licked the flesh one last time before dragging my tongue back up to her neck. "Fuck, Firefly. I think you liked me fucking your mouth almost as much as I did. You're so fucking wet."

"I did." She groaned and rode my hand, hips snapping as I pressed a knuckle against her clit. "I want to come so bad."

"I've got you. I'll always take care of this pretty pussy." I slipped two fingers inside her, grunting when I felt how soft and hot she was. Wanting that wrapped around my cock. But first, I needed to tease her. To wind her up. So I fucked her with my fingers, and I kept the heel of my hand against her clit as she rocked and jerked on me. Teased her nipples with my tongue and teeth until she became a writhing, whining, needy mess of girl flesh without words.

Once I had her exactly where I wanted her, I grabbed my cock and directed him inside her. Slammed home with a thrust so hard, her hips smacked against the wall and she cried out. And then I fucked her. Hard and fast, rough and unyielding, I fucked her against the tile, holding her in place with my body, pinning her hands above her head just as I'd imagined I would.

"Your mouth is a sweet sort of hell, but there's nothing like your pussy, Firefly. Nothing feels as good or as right." I slid almost all the way out, holding myself still with just the tip inside her. "Is this what you want? You want my cock buried deep, splitting you apart as I thrust home? You like me to take control and do what I want to you?"

She groaned what sounded like a yes, her hips jerking, trying to pull me deeper. I couldn't say no to her—never could. I plunged back inside, growling as I dropped a hand down to assault that clit the way I knew she liked. The way I knew would get her off.

And when she came—screaming my name with her head back and her body bowed—I followed, unable to hold back. Pressing deep inside her and filling her up. Good. So fucking good. So fucking mine.

I kept our bodies pressed together, holding her up as I caught my breath. As the feeling of rightness and bliss and want for more circled through my head. As she dragged her fingers along my spine and gave me goose bumps.

"I think we exhausted the hot water tank," Anabeth said, chuckling. I had to join her because yeah, we had. Cold water rained down on us, not that I'd given a single fuck for that. I'd been too busy to care, but now...

"Let's get out of here and find some clothes before we freeze."

"Good call," she said. But as soon as I shut off the water, she grabbed me and dragged me back for a long, slow kiss. The kind that would probably lead to us wrapped up in her bed again. The kind that made my exhausted cock stir. But when she broke it, the smile on her face seemed sad almost. Not at all what I'd been expecting.

"Anabeth?"

"Just...more that I missed." She snuggled closer, shivering as I wrapped my arms around her. "I missed how good we always were together."

Yeah, so had I. "Me too. Though, the first time wasn't so good for you. I thought it was amazing, but I think I lasted all of two minutes."

Her body shook as she chuckled. "Well...yeah. But that was to be expected. We got better."

"We did. And we will again." That was a promise I'd do anything to keep. I grabbed her hand and kissed her palm before tugging her out of the tub. "Let me get you dressed and warm."

She followed me into the bedroom, quiet but pliant. Clinging to me. I helped her into her yoga pants and a soft sweatshirt, even dropping to my knees to slide fluffy gray socks over her feet. And all the while, she stared at me, reaching out to touch as much as she could. Keeping us connected. I understood it too. I didn't want to be apart from her. Not at all.

But reality was coming in the form of my best friend, which meant I needed to not be naked when we left Anabeth's bedroom. I found my jeans from the night before easily enough, choosing to go commando underneath them. A clean, black tee I'd thrown in my jump bag did the rest of the job, then I dragged Anabeth down the stairs and toward the kitchen. She needed a cup of tea—she always needed a cup of tea.

But when we made our way into the kitchen, her hand squeezed mine almost painfully. Finn sat at the table, drinking a cup of coffee. Gage sat beside him with his long, thick survival knife resting on the table. The blade on that fucker put my Ontario Mark 3 to shame, hard and sharp-looking even from across the room. It was a knife for killing, for gutting and skinning.

"Morning," I said, heading for the coffeemaker. Anabeth let me go as she moved to fill her kettle, silent and almost distant all of a sudden. It had to be the knife. She'd just seen those scars on my body the night before—the knife had to be too much too soon.

Once I had my coffee made, I settled at the table next to Gage, kicking him for good measure. "Why don't you put that thing away?"

He grunted, glaring in my direction. "I was going to sharpen it."

"She doesn't need to see that."

"Why?"

"It's fine," Anabeth said, waving me off. "I understand it's a part of the job."

I didn't buy that, though. She still seemed off. Stiff. In fact, so did Finn. Neither of them seemed comfortable in their own skin.

"So," Anabeth said as she leaned a hip against the counter, her favorite mug in her hand. "What's the plan for today?"

Gage fielded that one. "We need to run recon in the woods. Make sure no one's hanging around out there. That's why I brought Finn. Figured he could guard the girl while we scouted."

The girl? Aw, fuck no. "She has a name."

"I do," Anabeth chimed in, raising her eyebrows over her mug. "I have a name. But considering I'm the only female in this group at the moment, I understand who *the girl* is."

Gage shot me a sarcastic sort of smirk.

"Jesus." I sighed and stretched back in the chair, the idea of roaming around the woods in the rain not exactly the most inviting thought. Especially after how I'd spent the last—I glanced at the clock—forty minutes. Ten minutes longer than I'd planned, but I wouldn't have traded a second of that time.

Gage grabbed his knife, flicking along the length of the blade with his thumbnail. "How far out should we go? All the way to the burn site?"

"What burn site?" Anabeth asked.

Shit, she still didn't know. "The Soul Suckers set up a meth lab on your property. We made sure to shut it down."

"Here?" She clutched the mug to her chest, her eyes big and round. "They set up a meth lab *here*?"

"Down on the eastern slope. There was an old barn Finn found out there. I'd never known—"

The crash of her mug hitting the wood floors stopped

everything, the pings as pieces landed the only break in the silence for three solid seconds. Shards of ceramic flew, chunks of white and tan littering the dark surface beneath our feet. And Anabeth stood in the middle of it, shaking. Trembling.

Looking more upset and scared than I'd ever seen her.

Chapter Sixteen

ANABETH

S hit." Bishop jumped to his feet, but I couldn't focus on him. Couldn't hear anything but the words reverberating in my head.

An old barn. Eastern slope. An old barn. Eastern slope.

I was going to be sick.

Suddenly, someone grabbed my elbow, tugging me away from the counter. Finn. His eyes the same deep blue-gray they'd been that day at the barn. So many years ago, so many lifetimes it seemed, and yet the same. So much the same. He wasn't smiling, though. Wasn't laughing. Not like that day. The one that destroyed my life.

The moment that took Bishop away from me.

Finn had his hands on me again, but this time, I was aware enough to yank away from him.

"Don't you touch me."

"Anabeth," Finn said, leaning forward. Reaching for me. So much like that day, like that moment in the barn when he'd almost killed me. When he'd killed the only good things I'd ever had in my shitty life.

I jerked away again, hissing as I stepped on a chunk of ceramic.

"Shit. Finn, back the fuck off." Bishop picked me right up off my feet, cradling me in his arms as he carried me to the other side of the counter. Away from the hurt and the mess. Away from his brother. But it was too late. The damage had been done. Years and years and years before, I hadn't paid enough attention. Hadn't done what I'd needed to, and there was no coming back from that. Just like the mug—my absolute favorite that I'd had since Miss had made it for me when I'd come to live with her—I was broken beyond repair.

"Put me down," I said, pushing Bishop away. Needing space. Needing air to breathe. Needing to get away. He did as I told him, watching me with wary eyes as he set me on my feet.

"You okay?"

"I'm fine." A lie—I was anything but fine. "I need to go take care of my foot."

"I'll help you," Bishop said, reaching for me. As if to protect me, to shield me. Too late, though. So many years too late.

"I've got this covered. Just...let me go."

Bishop did as I asked, looking hurt and confused. But I didn't have it in me to soothe him, didn't have the words or the heart to make him feel better when my own emotions had just been laid bare. There was only so much I could do at one time, and dealing with the sudden plunge into memories of the darkest days of my life took priority.

Finn closed the door behind himself, having stepped out onto the porch. Good. I didn't want to see him. Couldn't stand to look into those eyes so much like Bishop's and remember.

So I limped up the stairs, and I closed my bedroom door behind me. And I slid down the length of it to the floor, curled up in a ball, and sobbed for all the things I'd done wrong. For all the losses I'd suffered.

And for all the mistakes I could never, ever repair.

———

BISHOP

"What the fuck just happened?" Gage stood in the middle of the kitchen, staring at the door Finn had walked out of. Looking just as lost as I felt.

"No clue."

"That wasn't about a broken mug."

"No, it wasn't."

He grunted before bending to pick up the chunks of ceramic littering the floor. I should have helped him, but I couldn't stop watching the hallway Anabeth had disappeared down. Something was very wrong. And I needed to figure out what.

As if reading my mind, Gage said, "You want to finally tell me your history with that broad so I know what we're dealing with?"

Not in the slightest. I groaned, turning away from the hall as he dumped the ceramic pieces into the trash. "I really don't want to rehash shit."

"You haven't hashed yet. At least, not with me."

He was right. He was also my best friend. If anyone should know about Anabeth and me, it was Gage. The thought of telling him made my neck tight, though. "We dated."

"No shit."

"She was in high school—same grade as Finn and Elijah. She's older, though. Got held back one year because she couldn't keep up with all the moves." I shook my head, catching his questioning gaze. "She grew up in the foster care system. Miss was her grandmother, though she never knew Anabeth existed. Not until the kid was already a preteen and stuck in the system, bouncing from house to house to house."

"Fuck. That's—"

"Horrible? Yeah." Worse than horrible. That girl had been an emotionless stone when I'd first met her. A beautiful, unforgettable stone. "According to the stories, it was just as bad as you can probably imagine. But as soon as Miss found out about Anabeth, she hunted her down and brought her here. Finn and Elijah befriended her pretty easily, so she hung out at our house with them. That's how I met her."

"So you dated what...a couple years?"

"Almost four, yeah." A lifetime and yet it went so quick. And then came fourteen years of not having her. A thought that felt like a knife slicing through my chest. "That girl...she was my everything, my world. But I was at school, too fucking busy finishing up my double major in forestry economics and silviculture—"

"Show-off." Flat, deadpan, the word left me speechless. Sadly, Gage was not. "Seriously, man. Double major? What, you missed out on the chess club in high school or something?"

Jackass. "Not my fault I'm smart, dude." I shrugged, huffing a laugh and ducking as he threw a kitchen towel at my head. "Your aim is shit."

"And you're a nerd. Carry on. You were at school, and Legs was here with your brothers."

That sounded...not the way it should have. "She had other friends."

Gage could pull off a seriously dramatic eyeroll when he wanted to, and apparently, he wanted to. "Fine, she wasn't with your brothers. So what happened?"

I'd been asking myself that question for fourteen years. "I have no idea. One day, I got a phone call from her saying we were through and she was moving to Vegas. Done. End of story."

Gage looked about as confused as I'd always felt in regards to Anabeth walking away. "But why?"

"Don't know. I'm not ashamed to admit I was pretty fucking heartbroken. That girl had been my life for years. And when I went after her—"

"Because there was no way you weren't going after her."

"Exactly. But she was living with some guy. He answered the door."

"The fuck?" Gage stood there, staring, looking ready to rage. Ready to back me up.

Not that he needed to. "I didn't know it then, but she wasn't with him. He was a friend of Miss' and letting her stay at his place while she got settled."

"But she let you think he was more."

"Yeah." She had, and that still hurt. I headed for the table, needing to clear my head. To sit. To purge the thoughts dragging me down so I could see clearly. "That happened on a Wednesday. Alder was on leave, so he came to drag my sorry ass home after I found myself at the bottom of a bottle with nowhere to go or stay. I joined the Navy on Monday morning and ended up being accepted into the SEAL training program right away. So I finished my degrees and got the fuck out of town."

"And you never talked about her."

And admit I'd met—and lost—the woman of my dreams? Fuck no. I shook my head.

Gage huffed, sitting back in his chair. Balancing it on two legs. "And now she's a performer out in Vegas."

"Yeah. Tarot cards, tea leaf reading, psychic shit that's more intuition and knowing people than anything else. All the stuff Miss taught her."

"When's she going back?"

The question burned, the words embedding themselves in my chest like knives. Leave it to Gage to get right to the meat of the issue. "Doesn't matter."

The truth, but I couldn't deny that she *would* be going back. And soon. There was nothing for her in Justice. Nothing for her with me. She may have missed me all these years apart, but she'd never tried to get in touch. Never reached out. She'd missed me, just not enough to do anything about it. The only reason she'd come home was for Miss, and even then, she hadn't sought me out. I'd found her. I'd brought us right back to that place...and she would run again. But this time, I wouldn't give up chasing her.

"Rain's falling harder," Gage said, yanking me from the death spiral of my thoughts. I looked up, no longer able to see past the edge of the porch. The one where Finn stood, leaning his shoulder against the wall and looking out toward the woods to the east.

"You should take Finn back to town before you get flooded in here. I don't know what's wrong with him and Anabeth, but there's some sort of tension there."

"Yeah, I saw that myself." Gage came around the table, smacking my shoulder hard before squeezing it. "This girl makes you happy. Might be time to think about changing things in your life to accommodate hers. But no matter what, I've got your back, brother. Always."

There was nothing to say to that because I already knew I'd probably be making some big changes if I wanted to keep Anabeth in my life. I simply nodded, staring out the window as he headed outside and led Finn to his Jeep. As he backed out of the driveway and disappeared into the hazy afternoon rainstorm. I sat and looked out the window for what felt like hours as my determination sank in.

Ignorance was not knowing something; stupidity was learning

the same thing over and over without catching on. I'd been down this road with Anabeth, been left behind and hurt and damn near crushed by her. And there I was, ready to let her do it again.

I was as stupid as any man had ever been, but there was no stopping what I'd started. I'd fallen back in love with Anabeth, but it wouldn't matter. She was going to leave me. To leave Justice. And once again, she'd take my heart with her unless I figured out a way to convince her to let me go with her. But there were conversations to have before I could try for that, explanations needed. About why she left in the first place, why she'd broken my heart. Why she hadn't loved me enough then to find a way to work out whatever was going on with her.

To move forward, we'd have to go back. I didn't know if she was ready, though.

Or if she ever would be.

At least without one hell of a push from me.

Chapter Seventeen

ANABETH

I woke up warm and comfortable, wrapped in Bishop's arms with his solid weight beside me. The shadows lining the walls of my bedroom told me I'd slept much longer than I should have. I couldn't even remember coming to bed—the last thing I recalled was sitting with my back to the door and crying. Sobbing, really. Suffering as I deserved to suffer, even though I hated feeling so broken and worthless.

I didn't feel worthless in Bishop's arms, which scared the daylights out of me.

I rolled over to face him, looking into his deep, gray eyes and fighting the warm tug they had on my heart. "Hi."

He didn't speak, didn't smile either. Instead, he stared at me, a strange, almost detached expression on his face.

"Bishop?"

"You're going to head back to Vegas, aren't you?"

My heart stuttered, and my mouth went dry. "Yes."

A tic in his jaw gave away his anger, so I reached for him. Held on to his face as I tried to find the right words to explain.

"I have no job here, no way to make money. There's no real future for someone like me in Justice."

His eyes seemed to harden right in front of me. There was no stopping his anger, no calming it down. Before I could even try, he rolled away. Sitting up on the edge of the mattress, he rested his elbows on his knees and kept his back to me. Stiff and unyielding. Angry.

"No future with me, you mean."

His words landed like a lead balloon inside my stomach. "I didn't say that."

"Why'd you leave? That first time—why'd you run away from everything?"

From him. He meant from him. This wasn't a conversation I wanted to have. I couldn't deal with the disappointment if I told him the truth. The disgust. It was one thing to see his pain—to know I'd broken his heart. It was another to rip out that heart and leave it on the floor.

"I had to," I said, giving him nothing else.

His voice sounded hard and filled with rage when he asked, "Why?"

"Bishop—"

"Goddammit, Anabeth." He exploded off the bed, pacing back and forth. His steps heavy, his face angry. "Tell me why you left. I deserve to know the truth."

But I couldn't. I shook my head, every inch of me hating that I couldn't give him what he wanted. "Please don't ask me. I can't...I just can't."

Bishop finally stopped pacing, his head hanging low and his chest heaving as if he'd just run a marathon. Or he was dealing with a ton of pain. "I won't do this again."

The first tear hit my cheek followed closely by the second and the third. All the years apart, all the pain at being separated, at leaving him and forcing myself to try to forget—it came out in my tears. I'd never allowed myself to cry over Bishop, never given in to the urge. How could I when the pain was of my own making? But, now? So close to what I'd always wanted but still so far away? All I could do was cry.

"Anabeth—"

I shook my head, cutting him off. "I know."

Which was the wrong thing to say. He growled like a bear, long and loud and filled with a rage I deserved. "You don't know. You weren't here. You don't know how much of a mess you left me in. You destroyed me, Anabeth, and you don't even care."

Oh God, he was so wrong. So very, very wrong. "I care. I care so much."

"Then tell me why."

I shook my head, unable to stop the tears from falling. "You'd hate me. I hate me for what I did. I can't...I won't say it."

Bishop went quiet and still, his eyes losing their fire as he stared at me. As his shoulders curled in slightly, just enough for me to notice. A posture of defeat.

I'd broken him...again.

"I'm going to wait downstairs for Gage to come back," he said, his voice harsh and raspy. Cheap whiskey over ice instead of the usual sound of good bourbon.

"Okay," I whispered. Maybe later we could talk more, maybe he would listen to me when I told him he shouldn't know. When I tried to explain around what had happened. I didn't want to disappoint him again, and there was no way—

"Once Gage gets here, I'm leaving. He'll guard the house tonight."

My world screeched to a halt. He was leaving me. Fitting,

considering I'd been the one to run away from him, but this time... I'd sort of allowed myself to hope for more. For something. For things I knew better than to even want.

"Bishop, I'm sor—"

"No." Clipped, concise, completely robotic. Too pissed to show emotion. "I can't do this. I don't want to, Anabeth. Not again. Not without knowing the truth. It's the one thing I want, the one thing we need to be able to rebuild something that could be great, and you can't give that to me. I don't know what to do with that."

He turned and walked out of the room, leaving me behind this time. Leaving me to curl up with the pillow that still smelled like him and sob one more time for all the things we'd lost. All the things we could never get back.

For being such a coward.

———

Rex was one hell of a lap dog even though he was too big to be one. He was also a good dog to have around when your heart had been shattered into a million pieces.

"Who's a good boy?" I said, letting my voice go all soft and silly. The dog practically knocked me off the couch to snuggle, something I needed at that moment. Bishop had left hours ago, and...he hadn't come back. I'd expected him to. Truly thought he'd come walking back through the door at any second to try to convince me to stay or to change my mind or even just to fight with me.

Instead, I got nothing. But Rex...and Gage.

"All good." The man himself walked into the living room, causing my canine blanket to sit up, though he didn't leave me. Thank goodness, because being alone with Gage might have ranked right up there on the nightmare scale with being covered in spiders.

"Thanks for keeping an eye on things," I said as I patted Rex's side.

Gage frowned at his dog before shooting me a look. His eyes were darker than most—nearly black. The color so deep, they almost seemed dead or flat. Shye had called them sharklike, and I had to agree. But there was a spark there, something alive and interested. In what, I had no idea.

"You okay?" he asked, his voice deep. His tone direct.

Oh, his interest was in me. Or gossip about me and Bishop. Got it. "You really want me to get personal with you?"

"Not in the least, but you're my buddy's girl. I have to do what I can to make sure you're okay."

His words sliced across my chest like razors. "I'm not Bishop's anything."

Gage chuckled and leaned a hip against the fireplace, crossing his arms over his broad chest. "Both of you really suck at this. It's obvious he wants you and you want him... Quit fucking around."

"It's not that easy."

"Nothing worthwhile ever is."

My chest tightened, the truth choking me. "I can't...he'd never forgive me."

Gage continued to watch me, frowning.

At least, until he opened his mouth again. "You know they murdered Leah."

My breath caught. So blunt—no sugarcoating anything for this man. "Yes, but I don't know what that has to do with this situation."

"Life is short. Take every ounce of pleasure you can get, and fuck the rules."

Fuck the rules. "That's an interesting take on life."

"I'm an interesting guy."

I raised my eyebrows, letting the sarcasm drip from my voice as I replied, "And so humble."

"It's the SEAL in me. We're the best—no question."

"Alder might argue that fact. If I remember right, the man was a Green Beret."

"Alder can argue all he wants about his subterfuge skills and unconventional warfare tactics. In terms of brute force and getting shit done, SEALs are where it's at. We're the best." He snapped his fingers, causing Rex to jump up and pad across the room toward him. "I'm going to do another sweep outside before locking up for the night. Stay put, okay?"

"Yes, sir, Mr. SEAL, sir." I cocked a brow and gave him a totally inaccurate salute, to which he just rolled his eyes before strolling out the door. But his words lingered, his vivacity for life hovering in the air around me.

Life *was* short. I'd missed out on so much already—time with friends, with Bishop, with Miss. All because I couldn't bear to admit my sins to the man I loved. That fear had ruled me for over a decade, had left me grief-stricken and mourning for almost half my life. The three of swords card permeating my every move and thought. Stealing my chance at happiness.

How much longer would I allow it to take the things I loved away from me?

Too many thoughts weighed me down, and the only comfort I could think of was my old standard—a nice, strong cup of tea. I headed for the kitchen, letting my memories take over. Letting the pain flow through me that I normally fought off. That I tried not to remember.

As the water heated, I gave myself over to the grief of what I'd lost. I gave myself permission to feel that pain, even if just for a moment alone in the kitchen. Heart cracked wide open for once, I let the pain take me.

Having a baby would have been all wrong for us at the time, but losing her had destroyed everything.

When I'd found out I was pregnant with Bishop's child, I'd still been in high school. He'd still been in college. We'd been too young to deal with the responsibilities of becoming parents. And yet, as I stood there in the kitchen where I'd grown from teenager to woman, I couldn't stop my hand from resting on my belly.

The timing may have been off, but I would have loved that baby with everything I had.

I'd never truly gotten to mourn the life we'd created. Never gotten to deal with the possibility of having a child either. The baby had been gone before I'd even realized it was there, taken away from me because I'd been careless and stupid.

So very stupid.

I'd messed up one time, had made a decision that I'd known was wrong, and I'd lost our child because of it. How could I ever admit that to Bishop? How could he ever look at me again if he knew?

"No sense worrying over maybes," I muttered, remembering the words Miss had said a thousand times throughout my life. She'd helped me leave, had kept me from falling apart after the loss had caused me to shut down emotionally. She'd disagreed with my decisions, though. Had wanted me to stay in Justice, to tell Bishop what had happened, and to...I don't know. Wallow in the pain? Deal with the loss? It was too late to know at that point, though. Miss was gone. Bishop was gone. Our baby was gone. Meanwhile, I stood in Miss' kitchen, making another damn cup of tea to soothe my fragile soul. Alone. Always so alone.

Or perhaps not.

As I poured the water to steep the tea, a shadow at the window caught my attention. I glanced up, assuming it was Gage walking past as he'd been doing while on guard duty. I assumed wrong. Though I couldn't see through the glass due to the darkness and the rain outside, the shape was clearly all wrong. The height off and the shadow too thin. That wasn't Gage out there, which meant...

"Shit," I hissed, my hands shaking as I picked up my teacup. I needed my phone. Needed to call for help or find Gage or hide. Something. Anything. I tried to keep my face impassive, tried to pretend I didn't know someone lurked just on the other side of the glass. And I calmly, carefully walked back down the hall toward the stairs leading to my bedroom where I'd left my phone.

Calmly and carefully went flying out the window when I heard the crack of broken glass from behind me. I raced through the foyer instead. Five feet, four. Footsteps pounding behind me, urging me to run harder, faster. Three feet left. I reached for the newel post that anchored the stairway railing, knowing I still had to get all the way to the second floor. Foot on the first step, ready to leap to the third and...

I didn't make it.

Chapter Eighteen

BISHOP

The day had gone to shit. Ever since I'd left Anabeth's place, I'd done nothing but drive and stew and grow angrier with the world. The rain fell in sheets, the ditches and creeks I passed not able to hold back the waters any longer. Not that I gave a shit. Let it flood. Let the whole damn town get washed away so we could all start anew. There was nothing I could have wanted more.

And yet, that wasn't the truth. I didn't want the town to flood because that would cause hardships for the residents. Alder, as the oldest Kennard brother, ran shit, but I felt the responsibility we'd been born into just as strongly. Also, I *did* want something more than a fresh start for the town. I wanted a fresh start with Anabeth. I wanted her to stay, to be in my bed every night, to give us a chance at the life she'd walked away from over a decade before.

But she wasn't staying, which meant I wouldn't be getting what I wanted without giving up so much. Just another thing to sour my mood and make me want to keep roaming the streets like some sort of wraith.

My phone pinged with an incoming text, so I pulled over at the next road. No sense causing accidents when the rain would be doing enough of that. Once stopped, I swiped the screen to life.

House secure, girl upset. WTF did you do?

Gage, of course. Not Anabeth. I wasn't in the mood to deal with my best friend, so I tossed the phone across the seat and pulled back out into traffic. More driving, less sitting still.

The anxiousness, the need to run from the pain, overwhelmed me. I'd moved past those feelings, had learned to tuck my Anabeth memories away and not think about the pain she'd caused me. She'd ripped that wall down, though. Had yanked the memories right to the forefront of my mind and left them there, raw and hurting.

My Firefly, the heartbreaker.

"Motherfucker," I said as I turned back toward town. I wanted to hate Anabeth for bringing this on me, to curse her name and walk the fuck away from her for good, but I couldn't. My heart wouldn't let me. I knew I'd go back to her house, that I'd fight for her again and again and again. I had to—she was the other half of my soul, the one woman who'd ever seen the real me and simply loved me. I'd never give up on her.

Which, at that moment and in that situation, pissed me off even more.

Another ping for a text. I almost ignored it, almost left that phone lit up across the seat, but that sad, little weak spot inside me said it could be Anabeth. I pulled over again, and I reached for the phone. Swiped the screen that had long since gone dark back to life.

And I read the two words without comprehending them for a solid thirty seconds.

Ambush. Breached.

When their meaning finally sank in, my heart dropped.

Breached. Someone had made it into Anabeth's house. Had gotten past Gage and had my girl all to himself.

I slammed my foot down on the gas, cursing the fact that I'd again worn my dress shoes instead of my boots. I wasn't prepared for this at all, which threw my anger into downright rage.

"Hang on, baby. I'm coming." I performed a quick U-turn then gunned the engine, flying through the rain at a speed not safe for anyone. More than once, my tires slipped as I raced toward Widow's Ridge, but I held on to the wheel and kept myself on the road. I had to get there; I had to make it. My god, the things they could be doing to her. And Gage, my best friend and partner. I'd left him there to do *my* damn job. You never left your wingman alone—I knew that. I lived that rule, which was why Gage and Rex had been living with me. Why he'd even moved to Justice in the first place.

I'd fucked up all around on this one.

As I turned onto the road leading up to the ridge, I grabbed my phone again. We needed backup. I had no idea how many men had breached the house, but I didn't want to take a chance that we'd be outnumbered without sending out a call for support.

"Siri, call Alder cell."

"Calling Alder cell," the robotic voice returned just before the phone clicked and started to ring. One, two, three, four...voice mail.

"Shit." I waited for the message to finish before laying out the issues. "Hey, brother, we're going to need some help at Anabeth's. Gage is up there alone and sent me a text that they've been ambushed. At least one person has breached the house. I'm on my way there, going to park by Shye's old place and hike in so as not to be seen. Get your ass up here."

As I hung up, I thought about calling Deacon or Camden, but I was already coming up on the overflowing creek that had created a fast-moving stream right over the road. I hit it at a slower speed than I wanted, but it didn't matter. The water had risen deeper than when I'd come down the hill, and the current pushed my truck sideways before I was halfway across the swath.

I bit out a curse as I tried to hold on to the wheel, but there was no directing the vehicle. I was at the mercy of the water. Thinking ahead, I rolled down my window and unbuckled my seat belt, knowing if the truck ended up in a deep eddy, it would sink like a stone.

Luckily or not, the water didn't take me far. A tree stopped the truck with a jolt, making my teeth rattle almost as hard as the metal body itself. I didn't have time to recover, though. I was in motion before the rocking stopped, reaching for the bag of weapons I'd been carrying with me since before the grand opening at Katie's restaurant...

And coming up empty.

"Motherfucker."

The guns. The explosives. The night vision goggles. Even my boots. Everything sat back at Anabeth's place. I'd left in such a hurry, I'd forgotten to take my jump or weapons bag with me. The only thing I had in my truck was my standard-issue Ontario Mark 3 knife. Black and sharp with a six-inch blade and a handle almost made for my hand, the knife had been at my side since the day I'd joined the SEAL training program. I was almost more comfortable with it than my guns.

Almost.

At least, that's what I told myself as I shoved open the driver's door and stepped out into the knee-high water. The rain immediately soaked me to the skin, the wall of falling water restricting my sight lines, and the current pulled at my feet. My shoes gave me no traction, but I pushed through. Hanging on to the truck until I could grab the branches of the tree for support. Let the water come, let the flood cover me. I *would* make it through because my girl needed me to. My teammate needed me to. And nothing would stop me from getting to them.

With every step I took, the water dropped lower until it finally fell below my ankles. As soon as I felt balanced and no longer fighting the flow, I started running. Racing through the dark toward Anabeth and Gage. I stayed on the road instead of heading into the forest, unafraid of being caught. No one would be coming up this way unless they were on my team...or the enemy's. Either way, there'd be plenty of warning if a vehicle actually made it along the rocky excuse for a road. Besides, trying to run through the forest would slow me down. I'd move into the trees once I made it to the property. I wasn't looking to be a ghost, just to sneak the fuck in and beat down whoever had thought they were badass enough to go after my girl.

As I passed where the burned-out shell of Shye's trailer sat, I started chanting in my head. *One more mile, one more mile...*just one more mile to go. Seven minutes or so at a full run, ten in these conditions. Fuck, too long.

"Just hang on, baby. I'm coming for you."

Chapter Nineteen

ANABETH

My head ached, my ribs were likely cracked, and my arm burned where the bastard had grabbed me, but I was alive. Alive and alone with the asshole from the restaurant. The guy in the Soul Suckers vest with the patch that said Blade. The one I'd mocked with his tarot card.

Bad plan, Anabeth. Really bad plan.

Blade paced the foyer as he'd been doing for several minutes already, looking anxious and unsettled. Possibly high too. "You didn't come home alone. Where's the guy?"

I didn't answer, not sure if he meant Gage or Bishop. Either way, they weren't with me, so it didn't matter. I didn't have an answer. Though, if he meant Gage, that could be a good sign. It meant he hadn't killed Bishop's best friend. Meant I still had a chance to get out of this unscathed. Well, as unscathed as possible considering how the bastard had picked me up and thrown me to the floor. I was hurting, but I hoped I'd find the strength and speed to get away when the time came for me to run. Because it would come, and if I let the pain of some measly cracked ribs slow me down, I wouldn't make it out of this alive.

"I asked you a question, bitch."

I still wasn't answering. In fact, I lifted my chin and glared at him, refusing to back down.

I didn't expect the slap in the face he delivered.

Pain erupted behind my eye and sliced across my lip, and the crack of his hand meeting my face echoed through my head. The force of the blow knocked me right off the step I'd been sitting on. I fell to the floor, wincing and fighting to hold back my tears. The bastard had hit me without reserve, had intended to hurt and scare me with that move. Well, he could keep slapping me. I wasn't crying because of it, and I wasn't answering him. Couldn't. If the guy didn't know where Gage was, I wasn't going to give him any information. And Bishop...well, Bishop had left me, but Blade didn't need to know that.

Gage. I needed to focus on Gage. He wouldn't let anything happen to me—not really. If he was still alive, he'd find a way to help me. To get me out. Not because he was a charitable, kind soul, but because I was Bishop's in his eyes. I was Bishop's girl, and Bishop was Gage's best friend. He'd do anything to save me because, deep down, it was the same as saving Bishop.

I just had to be patient. Maybe. I hoped. At least Blade didn't have a gun. Not from what I could see, anyway.

Oh god, what if he has a gun?

Before I could wrap my head around that new terror, Blade dropped into a crouch before me, glaring. Looking ready to kill. "Last time, bitch. Where's the guy?"

Silence. I just had to be patient. This was bad, it was really bad, but Gage would help me. He'd track down Bishop. The two would—

Blade pulled a wicked-looking knife from behind his back, one that was long and thick with serrated edges and a curve to the tip that looked as if it would slip under my skin with ease. The sight made my heart skip a few beats as two thoughts slammed into me at once.

The name on his patch fit.

And things had just gotten a hell of a lot worse.

Chapter Twenty

BISHOP

I crept up on the house after way too fucking long running. I'd never wished for my uniform boots more than I did in those moments when I'd been slipping and stumbling through the woods. The flat bottoms of my dress shoes simply couldn't stand up to the demands of racing through the dark over wet leaves and grass. Should have worn fucking spikes.

The rain hadn't stopped. It continued to drown the mountain in a deluge of water. For once, I was thankful for it, though. That downpour helped hide the sound of every footstep as I moved closer to the Hansen house. As I started jogging through a perimeter check.

Keeping tucked as far into the shadows as I could, I circled Miss' property through the tree line at the back. The deeper forest on that side meant it would be easier to hide if I came upon someone. Not that I'd want to hide, but with only a knife for a weapon, my options were limited if I had to go up against more than one guy.

The back door stood open, obviously the point of entry. Whoever had breached the building had probably kicked it in. No way had Anabeth or Gage left it unlocked and wide open like that. But the door wasn't the only thing wrong with the picture before me—two guys guarded either corner of the house, making it nearly impossible to sneak inside. I wasn't out of options, but I was definitely in a difficult situation.

I still needed to see what was happening around the front, though. As much as I had the urge to race inside the house like the Lone fucking Ranger, I couldn't. I had no guns, no way to protect myself or Anabeth without getting real close to whoever had her. I couldn't take that risk.

Slinking farther along and heading east, I spotted a third man leaning against the house right under Miss' bedroom window. He looked bored, his attention anywhere but on the woods where I stood. A weak link in their defense. Standing outside in the rain wasn't any fun for sure, but Gage and I could do it for days if necessary. That guy looked ready to bolt at any second. The other two—the ones guarding the north and south sides of the house—not so much.

Moving as quickly as I could, I continued on my way, checking for others. I even tried to get an idea of what was happening inside, but the rain obscured my vision, and the curtains over the front windows blocked my view into the house. I needed to find Gage. I needed to rescue Anabeth. I also needed to get my damn hands on a weapon. I could handle two men easily enough with a gun, especially with that guard under the windows appearing completely useless. Four was a different story. That required a little more planning. Backup would be nice, and having my partner by my side would be even better. Plus, Gage might shoot my ass if he didn't know it was me creeping through the woods. Best to find the cranky fucker and fast.

A shadow suddenly moved toward me, causing me to jump and pull my knife. Rex, looking way too fucking happy to see me, trotted through the darkness. Wet—soaked, really—and as silent as his fucking owner, the dog came right to my feet and wagged his tail. I didn't need to find Gage. He'd found me through his dog.

I knelt down to rub his head. "What are you doing here, boy?"

Rex turned to look behind him before taking two steps back, returning his focused gaze to mine. I'd watched enough *Lassie* episodes as a kid to know the jokes about that damn dog barking and making a scene to get the little boy to follow her. Rex wasn't much of a scene-maker, but his point was clear. *Follow me.* So I followed a damn dog through the pitch-black woods until we reached Gage's Jeep. I'd missed it on my first go-round because he'd buried it well beneath the trees alongside the shed on the west side of the property. Smart man.

"How'd you train Rex to come get me?" I asked once I found my friend in the dark.

"You ever watch *Lassie*?"

"Yeah."

"Me too." He went quiet, ending the conversation. Going back to staring out across the yard toward the house. I followed his gaze but saw nothing unusual. Nothing that would make us pause. Nothing standing in our way except the two guys on guard duty. But if he felt the need to wait, there would be a reason for it.

"Situation?" I asked, almost not wanting to know.

"All fucked up. Big guy from the restaurant—road name Blade —is inside with Anabeth."

I gripped my knife harder. "She okay?"

Gage didn't answer. There were a couple of reasons for that, I figured. Either he knew she was okay and thought that was a stupid question; he knew she wasn't okay and didn't want me kicking his ass for not protecting her; or he wasn't sure and...fuck, I had no clue why he wouldn't just say that. Knowing Gage the way I did, option two was out. The man would have given his life for Anabeth's simply because he didn't like bringing women into war. My connection to her would have solidified that decision. If he was allowing Blade to breathe the same air as Anabeth, it was because he had a reason. The first option was also unlikely—Gage wouldn't waste a second telling me how stupid I was. The third...well, the third made me want to race into that house blind to get to my girl.

Gage spoke before I could take my first step. "Last I saw, Blade had her in the foyer and was pacing pretty intensely. I figure we've got about three minutes to get in there before the answer to if she's okay moves into the probably-not range."

Motherfucker. My heart stopped, restarting in a pounding rhythm. If he hurt her...if he killed her... I couldn't even think it. Couldn't allow myself to picture a world without her in it without wanting to run inside, to hell with the fact that it'd be a suicide mission. The smart thing to do was wait for the path to be clear. It was also the hardest.

I pointed to the northwest corner of the house where one of the guards stood. He'd spot us if we made a run for the front door. Even with only half-decent aim, he likely would shoot one or both of us. He'd also raise a shit-ton of noise and give away our approach.

"We need to take out the eyes around the house. Especially that guy."

Gage didn't even blink. "Already on it."

"How?"

"Deacon. Called him in as soon as I texted you, but he was closer and made it up the mountain a lot quicker. You took fucking forever."

Yeah, I did. "My truck got swamped in the creek. I had to run for it."

"You should run more. Your time is shit."

Someday, I'd wring his neck. Today was not that day. "Okay, jackass. Let's get off my speed and back to the issue of some guy holding my woman hostage. What's the plan?"

"Deacon's in the air. He'll take out the guy in our way. Once he's done, we go in." He cocked his head, his brow furrowing as he thought something through. "Well, unless we reach that three-minute mark first. Two minutes at this point."

I tightened my hold on the knife, looking out across the yard and waiting for a sign that it was time to move. I would never forgive myself for walking out that door if anything happened to Anabeth. Never. Which meant I needed to get her the fuck out of there and away from this Blade guy.

Two minutes was too long.

"So Deacon takes out the guy on the northwest corner back there. There are two more on the east side—one parallel to that guy, and one farther up, almost to the front of the house. Plus, we've got Blade inside."

"That's on us. We take Blade out while Deacon finishes off the guys outside."

So just one. We could handle one in our sleep, even with me only having a knife for a weapon. "Bust in and hit him hard?"

"Is there any other way?"

Yeah, there was. Sniping the fuckers before they even knew you were there. Deacon Manns was one of the best at that shit. I loved ribbing my brother—the Army Special Forces hero—about the Green Berets not being as good as us SEALs, but the truth was, Alder and Deacon were a couple of smart soldiers. In a situation like this, where stealth, subterfuge, and silent assassination were our best bets, Deacon was the first person I would have called. After Gage. Because that silent, broody motherfucker had fought by my side for a lot of years. And we were about to do the same again.

Less than a minute until go time.

"I've only got my knife." I inched forward. Ready to attack. Adrenaline racing through my bloodstream. "Left my ammo bag in the house."

Gage didn't blink, simply pulled a gun from the holster on his hip and handed it to me before watching the house again. Intense, focused, and ready for action. I figured we had thirty seconds left before we were going in whether the guard on the northwest corner was still breathing or not.

A single pop sounded, breaking the constant drone of the rain. It wasn't loud—most likely not even heard in the house—but there was no mistaking what had just happened. Especially when the guard in our way suddenly fell to the ground. Deacon, former Special Forces sniper and current bar owner, had just taken out our first target. Time to act before the other two figured that out.

I tucked my knife under my belt and gripped the gun Gage had given me, ready to get this over with. To get my girl out of there. Without a signal, without a fucking word, we took off for the house at a run. Gage and I moved as one silent unit, not needing to speak to know the plan. Use the darkness and the rain to cover our approach, bust the front door down, save the girl, and kill the bad guy. Easy, except the girl held my heart in her hand, and if anything happened to her—

"Bishop."

I stopped and raised my weapon, unable to figure out why Gage had called my name when we were so close to the porch. "What?"

"If she's down...if I was wrong about the three minutes...I'm sorry."

Down...dead. Fuck, I'd never felt so close to a heart attack in my life.

Gage looked pained, almost unsure of himself. Not like the Gage I knew at all. Neither was apologizing. The man had never apologized for shit. I knew he understood how much Anabeth meant to me, knew he'd do anything for her, but he'd waited for me. He'd done exactly what I would have in the same situation. If he'd rushed in there without clearing the guards, he'd be dead. And so would she.

She might be anyway.

"Get me in the fucking door, man. We'll deal with the rest once we're inside."

She'd better be alive.

I slipped the rest of the way to the door, taking my spot on the right side as Gage stepped squarely in front of it. We'd broken down doors before—we'd probably do it again at some point. This was the easy part.

Not getting shot once we'd made it inside was harder.

Gage gave me a look—making sure I was ready—before he raised his foot and kicked forward. The wood frame didn't stand a chance against his assault. The door busted through the jamb and swung open, wood and glass flying all around and scattering across the floor. I was inside before the useless piece of wood hit the wall behind it, stomping my way through the foyer.

Blade had turned when the boom of Gage's foot hitting the door sounded, but he was slow to react. He was also not prepared for us, because he froze for just a second as I hurried toward him with my gun pointed at his face. That's when his knife hit the floor, and my world went red. He was going to cut her? To slice into her skin and make her bleed?

Out of my peripheral vision, I could see Anabeth huddled against the stairs behind him, could almost sense the fear radiating off her. That, along with the image of that knife slicing through her pale, soft flesh did me in.

This fucker had to go.

But he wasn't slow or stupid, though he *was* suddenly unarmed. A fact he came to realize just in time. Before I could reach him, he grabbed Anabeth and pulled her to her feet. Using her as a shield, hiding like a coward behind her body.

Motherfucker. "You've got five seconds to decide if you're ready to die."

"You shoot, and you hit the girl."

He wasn't wrong, but he wasn't completely right either. I could have taken a shot. Could have aimed slightly wide of her to hit him in the neck, face, or shoulder. Hell, when I'd been in the military, I *had* taken that shot. More than once. I could hit my target.

But Anabeth's eyes met mine, so wide and blue and scared that I couldn't risk her. Couldn't take that chance. Another color caught my attention, though. A deep red quickly turning purple on the side of her face. A bruise. Blade had hit her.

I was going to gut him like a motherfucking fish.

"You're going to regret ever stepping into this house," I said, keeping my eyes on his. Gage grunted behind me, probably with his gun still drawn on the two. A situation I needed to deal with. I took my finger off the trigger, widened my arms and pointed my gun to the ceiling, then moved to set it down. "Disarm, Gage."

Another grunt, but he followed my lead, setting his handgun next to mine on the foyer table. Far enough away that Blade couldn't get to them before us.

The jackass hiding behind Anabeth grinned as if he'd won something. "You the big, bad military guys we keep hearing about? Don't seem so tough to me." He pulled Anabeth closer, nuzzling her neck and breathing his last breaths against her skin. "*This* is your hero, Firecrotch? Because if you were pinning all your hopes on him, you picked the wrong guy."

Anabeth looked right at me, still so obviously scared but also fierce. Brave in the face of her fear. Refusing to back down. "He's never been the wrong guy."

I stayed quiet, watching. Waiting him out. He'd make a

mistake—the guy was too twitchy not to. He probably assumed his team of guards would back him up. The way he kept darting his eyes toward the open door behind me, I could guess he expected them to come barreling in to deal with Gage and me any second now.

The thought made me smirk. "You waiting on someone?"

He flicked his eyes to meet mine, looking more nervous with every second that passed. "I'm not alone here."

Gage leaned a shoulder against the wall, pulling out his hunting knife to calmly, patiently clean the dirt out from under his thumbnail. "I'm pretty sure you are at this point. Wouldn't you agree, Bishop?"

I nodded, refusing to release Blade from my stare. "Totally. See, you made the mistake of coming to Justice with bikers. You can't win against the firepower we have here with that sort of crew."

"What, you got some sort of killing machine out in the woods?"

"Nah, just a sniper up in the trees."

His face went pale, and his arms dropped from Anabeth's. I saw my chance, and I wasn't letting him get his hands on her again. I dove for them, grabbing Anabeth and tossing her behind me toward Gage. He'd keep her safe, get her the fuck out of the house if she needed to escape. My focus stayed locked on Blade.

"You never should have touched her," I said, crouching low and prepping for a little hand-to-hand combat. "I wouldn't have let you live either way, but that bruise on her cheek means I'm going to make it hurt."

He didn't seem impressed. "Fuck you."

"No thanks. My dick belongs to her." I lunged and struck, my fist connecting with his jaw in a way that nearly knocked him off his feet. I took the opportunity to pull my knife, wrapping my fingers around the thick, black handle. I liked guns. I liked explosives too. But I excelled at knife fighting. Silent, sneaky, and able to be finished with an enemy in seconds right under the nose of their partners—something about that spoke to me.

And something about my knife in my hand made Blade's eyes go big.

"Gage, move," I called as I went in for the kill. I really hoped he shielded Anabeth, that he covered her eyes or took her outside or... something. Anything. I didn't want her to see this, but it had to be done.

My first strike landed almost exactly as I'd planned—hard and deep, just to the side of the man's abdomen. He spun and swung his fist, but I won the battle in terms of speed. Ducking low, I pulled my knife and struck again before the blood had time to soak his shirt. Again before the first red drops hit the floor. And I just kept moving —staying out of his reach until I had a good shot at making contact, moving with him when he tried to bulldoze me and knock me down, stabbing in the good spots every chance I could find.

Though they were only the good spots if you wanted someone to bleed to death...quickly.

Blade wasn't going down without a fight, but he had no weapon, no real skills, and a brute force that exhausted quickly. In the end, I knelt over his body, his blood pooling on the floor and splattered across my chest. His eyes blank and staring. And my knife —the same one I'd been given as a newbie SEAL recruit—sticking out of his chest where I'd plunged it into his heart.

Mission accomplished.

I yanked the knife out of Blade's chest and rose to my feet just as Deacon came strolling in from the kitchen with what looked like a bag of chips in his hands. Eating. The man had just killed three people, walked in on another body on the floor, and he was eating. He didn't even blink as he took in the room.

"We're gonna need some serious disposal," he said before shoving another handful of chips into his mouth.

I grunted and backed up, shaky as the adrenaline wore off. Anabeth...my sweet, beautiful girl...stood just behind Gage. Her eyes locked on me. Looking absolutely terrified. *Fuck.*

"I say we use a chipper at the mill," Gage said, stepping away from Anabeth and frowning down at Blade's body. "We can burn the pieces after."

"So long as it's done," I said, still staring at Anabeth. Unable to look away. Scared to death that the fear on her face when she looked at me would never leave. But something about my voice or my words seemed to bring her out of herself. He face pinked up a little, and her eyes calmed. Her body settling slightly. Still uncomfortable, but no longer terrified. I'd take that.

"We should move," Gage said, bending to grab Blade's arms. "Deacon can stay as guard. My Jeep might be the only vehicle capable of crossing the road at this point. I really don't want to get stuck in a flooded creek while sitting on four bodies."

No doubt, and no need to worry about my truck. The vehicle could be replaced. The girl watching me couldn't. She never had been replaceable.

I wanted to ask Anabeth if she was okay, but I knew that answer would have to be no. How could she be after seeing what we'd done? I wanted to soothe her, to wrap my arms around her and pull her close. To protect her. But I was covered in blood, and there were bodies to deal with.

Soothing would have to wait, and I had no idea what her mind would come up with about me during that time. Other than that I'd failed at one simple task—keep her safe. The bruise on her cheek proved that.

As the guilt of failing her flowed through me, as Deacon and Gage scuttled out the front door with Blade's body hanging between them, I approached the one woman I knew I could never live without. The one who now might not ever be able to see me as anything other than a killer.

"We'll handle this mess. You go make some tea—it's going to be a long night."

She stared up at me, silent, her eyes so damn wary. But then she nodded. A simple head movement that brought her fiery red hair over her shoulder. I reached out, unable not to, and wrapped a single lock around my finger before tugging lightly.

"Be safe, Firefly. I'm coming back for you."

Chapter Twenty-One

BISHOP

No matter what horror movies and novels claimed, wood chippers were *not* the most convenient way to dispose of dead bodies.

"I need about six more showers," Gage said, rubbing his hand roughly over his bushy hair as he stared out the windshield.

"Maybe if you shaved now and again, you wouldn't feel so filthy."

"Women love a beard."

I wouldn't know, seeing as how I hadn't grown one in a few years, but I didn't give a fuck about women anyway. Just the one woman sitting back at the house we were slowly heading toward. The one who might not want to see me again—bearded or not.

When he hit the road leading up to the ridge, Gage went silent. Focused on the nonexistent path that would take us to Anabeth's. Water still covered the road, the rain feeding the overflowing creek, but the flow wasn't as fast as before. It wasn't as bad as when I'd driven through and lost my truck to the force.

"One of the earthen dams upstream must have broken," I said, nodding toward the evidence of a wider, faster body of water moving across the gravel. "That's why I couldn't make it across the stream."

Gage grunted, downshifting as the Jeep crawled through the water. "Looks like it. Wonder what's going on in town."

I checked my phone. "Nothing from Alder or Finn."

Gage kept driving, kept us moving. Kept holding his tongue and focusing on the road. Until...

"Text Katie. Make sure she's okay."

I didn't argue, pulling up her info and typing out a message as he'd asked, but there was no way I could just let that slide. "You sweet on our restaurateur?"

He didn't answer, which only made me more curious. And cautious.

"She's the sheriff's niece."

"I know that."

Good. It needed to be a consideration. "Just making sure you know. Their relationship could be a problem for you."

Gage kept his dark eyes on the road, his face set in a tight, angry expression. "There'll be no problem. I'm just looking out for the newbie."

There was no way I was buying that horseshit.

But as we finally made it through the water flowing over the road, I set aside my thoughts about Gage and Katie to focus on what was truly important to me. Anabeth. I needed to know that she was okay, that she'd calmed down since we left her. That Deacon had taken care of her without *taking care* of her. The man had charm—anyone would agree—and though I trusted him, Anabeth was mine. Some sort of primal, animal urge to mark her, claim her, and keep her all to myself flowed through me whenever I thought of her with someone else. Something I should probably push down until I convinced her to stay.

Or convinced her to take me with her when she left.

Leaving Justice for good had never seemed like an option before, but after the past few days? After Blade had taken her hostage? After even the thought that she might not have made it out of that house alive? There was no way I was letting her go without a fight. One that hopefully didn't end in bloodshed.

Deacon opened the front door as we pulled up in the Hansen driveway, leaning a shoulder against the jamb and watching us with a slight smile on his face.

"She drinks a lot of tea," he said, his eyes on mine when I stepped out of the Jeep.

"Always has. So did Miss."

He shrugged, switching his focus to Gage. "We all good?"

"Yeah." Gage climbed onto the porch, running his hand over his wet hair again. "I've got a couple little things to deal with, but those four won't be telling any tales."

"Good." Deacon nodded and stepped out onto the porch. "I think you need some time with your girl, Bishop. Or maybe she needs time with you."

Yeah. I definitely needed that. "You two sticking around?"

"Nah," Deacon said, shaking his head. "Gage and I will take Rex out for breakfast."

My lips kicked up in a smile, and I darted a look at Gage. "To Katie's?"

Deacon shrugged, looking like he knew exactly what he was planning. "Yeah. It's close enough, and they've got good food. Plus, she doesn't seem to mind the mutt running around her restaurant. You down, man?"

"Could eat," Gage said, not looking at either of us as he nodded.

Too stiff to be casual. The man wanted to do more than eat, but he wasn't admitting it. He whistled, and Rex came racing out from the hallway, jumping and slobbering all over his owner.

"So," I said, focusing on my friends instead of the mutt at my feet. "You two are going to breakfast, and I'm—"

"Walking the plank." Gage smirked.

Accurate. "Jackass."

Deacon chuckled and smacked my shoulder as he walked past me. "She's something else, that's for sure. I can see why you're stuck on her. Good luck, man."

I had a feeling I'd need it.

Gage bumped into me, holding on to my elbow as he did. Supportive but putting me in my place. "Now I know why you never dated redheads. She's pretty fucking unforgettable."

I huffed, knowing there was no way to deny that fact. "Completely."

He stared hard, his face serious, his hand steady on my arm. "I'm glad I didn't fuck up and get her killed."

That was about as close to emotional as I'd ever seen the man.

"Me too." Understatement. Because if she'd died last night? My world would have ended right there where it had truly begun.

Gage gave me a clap on the shoulder then stepped out into the rain, following Deacon across the driveway. They left me alone on the porch, heading off for food and time with the little brunette who'd moved back to town. Me? I was more interested in the redhead inside the house.

I stared through the open door for a handful of long minutes—nerves firing and anxiety creeping higher, almost drowning me. But like when the water busted over the road, there was no way through but forward. No way to know if she could get past what I'd done to Blade if I didn't deal with it head on. No way to convince her to stay with me if I didn't fight.

So I put one foot in front of the other, stepped inside, and closed the door behind me.

Chapter Twenty-Two

ANABETH

Cleaning the blood of a dead man who'd pulled a knife on you off your grandmother's wood floors had never been on my list of things to do before. Doing it while trying not to show fear to the friend of your ex who'd killed the man was about as bad as it sounded. And exhausting. The alternate reality I'd found myself in really sucked except for the fact that Bishop would be coming back to see me soon. Or at least, I hoped he would. God, if he didn't—

"Another cup of tea? You're going to float away from us." Deacon—handsome, charming, and way too smooth for the likes of Justice—shot me a teasing grin across the kitchen table. I didn't return it.

"Tea calms me."

And it did usually, but not then. I'd been in the kitchen since we finished bleaching the floor. I'd made my first cup while Deacon had been outside, burning our bloody clothes and towels. As the hours had passed and Bishop hadn't returned, I'd kept drinking. I was on cup number eight. Maybe nine.

I was also out of my favorite tea.

I clung to that last mug, almost afraid to take a sip. Not wanting the comfort it offered me to end. I'd always liked minty teas. They had been a link to Bishop. He'd been chewing spearmint gum the day I met him, had been doing it again the first time he'd kissed me. When I left him, I couldn't listen to the music that reminded me of us or watch the movies and TV programs we'd watched together. But the spearmint...the warmth inside of me as I drank the tea that tasted like him...that stayed. It became a constant in my life. A little bit of Bishop with me no matter where I went. And it was about to end for this trip because Bishop might not ever want to talk to me again.

The thought gutted me, left me unable to think or do or pay attention to anything as the tea in the mug grew cold. As Deacon came and went. As the light began to peek over the mountains and brighten the morning sky.

As Bishop suddenly appeared in the entryway to the kitchen.

Big and tall, with rough edges that counteracted Deacon's smooth ones, Bishop stole all the air from the room before breathing it back in. Something like calm settled over me as I sat there under his steely gaze. Something familiar and comfortable. Something I would hate to give up if he didn't forgive me for what I knew I finally had to tell him.

"I know that had to be scary," he said, looking almost stuck. As if I would kick him out instead of invite him in. I did that to him—made him doubt. That was all on me.

I hated myself sometimes. "It was very scary."

He nodded, hanging on to the wall. Bracing himself as the muscles in his biceps bulged. He stood and he blocked the door and he stared. And he dropped words like bombs in the quiet of the kitchen.

"I don't like killing."

My stomach knotted as I took a sip of the too-cool tea to grab hold of one last little bit of calm before I dove in.

"Yeah, well—you killed for self-defense." I set the mug down, my hand already shaking. "I don't have the same excuse."

His brows dropped, and his shoulders relaxed. Not a ton, but enough. He was with me. Paying attention. "What do you mean?"

And there it was. My opening...my chance to lay everything out. To tell him the truth and deal with the repercussions of it. To atone for my sins. The words were hard to find after so many years of hiding them, though. Almost impossible. At least at first.

"Anabeth?"

Sink or swim time.

"Finn started using drugs right after Thanksgiving of our senior year. At least, that's when I knew he was using." A hard, sharp pang of guilt washed over me at the shock on his face. They hadn't known —from what I'd found out later, Finn hadn't told his family he had a problem until much later. Months. By then...

"Okay." Bishop inched closer, coming to sit down in a chair beside me. Keeping his distance, though. The space between us yawned, and his eyes went flat and wary. "We didn't find out until late that summer."

"I know."

"You were gone by then."

"I kept in touch with a few people, and Finn...wrote me letters."

Bishop nodded, looking so damn hurt. A man reliving the time he'd spent sliding into hell. By then, he'd tracked me down in Vegas. Had come to find out why I'd left him. I'd slammed the door in his face, both literally and figuratively.

And that wasn't the worst of it.

"You came home for spring break that year," I said, letting myself remember. For once allowing the happiness to creep through the sad. "You told me you wanted to marry me."

He clenched his hand into a fist. Pulling himself away even more. "I did."

It was time. But even as I felt sure of that, as I stared down at the old tabletop, unable to look him in the face for this one, the words were just so hard to say.

My voice was rough when I said, "We made a baby that week."

I felt more than saw him recoil, something that forced my eyes to his even as they burned with the tears I did my best to hold back. The look on his face, the surprise. The pain. It half killed me, so I rushed on.

"I didn't find out... I wouldn't have kept it a secret, but by the time I knew..."

"You were gone." Hard and angry, his words hit me like a physical blow. Knocking me back in my chair. So wrong and yet not harsh enough. Not for what I'd let happen. For what I'd done.

"No," I said, breathing deep and fighting to keep the sick from rising in my throat. "By the time I knew, I'd already killed her."

Bishop lurched to his feet, his chair flying across the room as he stumbled back. "You had an abortion without talking to me?"

"No," I said, shaking my head and closing my eyes against what I knew was coming. What I knew had to be told. "I wouldn't have done that."

What I'd done hadn't been much better.

"Then what, Anabeth?" Bishop sounded almost crazed. Pissed off and likely unsure where to focus that rage. "You tell me you were pregnant with my child and you killed it... What the fuck happened? What was so bad that you had to run away from me and never talk to me about it?"

"Finn was using—"

"I know that," he roared.

I looked up, meeting his gaze. Needing to have his full attention for my confession. "And so was I."

Bishop froze, staring at me with his mouth hanging open. Every inch of him tense but restrained. On a leash. "You what?"

There was no prettying up this part. "It wasn't as often or as much, but I...I hung out with him a lot. We used sometimes. It made me feel better when I was missing you."

"So this is my fault."

"No, it's fully mine. But I want you to understand. I hated being here without you. I never tried to hold you back, though. I didn't want to get in your way. So I waited, and I filled my time with what I could to keep me sane."

He paced, his steps fast and strong. His path too short for such a wide stride. Like some sort of caged animal. "How long?"

The drugs. Of course he'd want to know more about the drugs.

"Almost a year before I got clean. Miss' friend that took me in—he wouldn't work with me if I was high, and I wanted to perform, so I stopped. Went to rehab. Did all the things he told me I had to do, all the things Miss wanted me to do. Except one. I didn't come back here. I couldn't face any of you after what happened."

Bishop sat back down, heavy. Tired. Still keeping so much distance between us. A distance that left me trembling for his touch.

"Jesus, Anabeth. I would have helped you."

"I know that. But by then...the guilt consumed me. I was so ashamed of what I'd done. What I'd lost for us." I shook my head, wiping away the cold, wet trails under my eyes. The tears I had no right to cry. "I couldn't face you."

He inched closer, dragging his chair around the side of the table. Making my heart skip a beat. "How did you lose the baby?"

Oh God. The one confession I hated to make above all others. The memory that ate at me every day, that never let me rest, that gave me nightmares. The decision that had almost killed me. But it was time—he deserved the truth. The whole story, even the ugliest parts.

"The old barn...the meth lab you burned down? It's been there for a long time. Finn found it one summer, and we sort of made it our secret place. He and I used to hide out down there senior year, getting high and hanging around like it was some sort of clubhouse." A clubhouse with lighters and cigarette papers, needles and rubber tubing. All the things we needed to chase that euphoria we couldn't find any other way. At least, until I took it too far. "One day, Finn got this new meth—said it was too good to smoke and that we had to inject it. So I did. I never even questioned him."

"You overdosed?"

If only. "No. I had a seizure, and my heart stopped beating. Technically, I died."

Bishop jerked back, fists raised as if to throw a punch. He closed his eyes, whispering a rough, "Jesus, Anabeth," before shaking his head.

Every inch of me hurt, my body trembling and cold. *Not yet*, I told myself. *You can break when you're done, but not yet.*

"I'm thankful that Finn got me help. To this day, I don't know how I made it, but I did. I woke up in a hospital bed and thought I was so lucky, that I'd finally reached the bottom and could use that to make a fresh start. I could get clean and do all the right things again. And I had plans to tell you about the drugs and the seizure—I really did. But after I was stabilized and aware of what was going on, this doctor came in looking so angry. He stood there at the end of my bed and berated me for being so irresponsible. He told me how I'd been pregnant, but that I wasn't anymore. That I'd lost the baby when I'd..."

I couldn't say it. Couldn't admit even to him that my drug use had cost us our child's life. All I could do was sit and sob for everything that one decision had cost me. My future, my family, my child, Bishop—everything. The guilt swamped me, left me drowning in a sea of emotions too rough to traverse. Too cold to survive. And Bishop...if he walked away as I'd always assumed he would, if he now saw me as something wretched and cruel, he would take my heart with him. Fully and completely. There would be no more future, no more chances, no more possibilities. There would be no more hope in my world.

But Bishop didn't leave. He didn't make a sound either. He sat and he stared at me and he stayed so still, I almost didn't know what to do.

And he made me scream when he wrapped his arms around me and lifted me into his lap.

Chapter Twenty-Three

BISHOP

My God, this girl. So much. She'd been through *so much* while I'd been away at school. And I'd had no idea. None. I'd failed her. I'd been careless with the one person I should have been cautious with. Been off doing my own thing—pushing myself to the brink to finish quickly instead of taking my time. Leaving her alone for my brothers to keep an eye on instead of waiting or figuring out a way to keep us together. I'd known her past—I'd always known that drugs and addiction were a part of her family story. I'd never thought they'd touch her again, though. I'd never thought she'd fall under their spell. I'd been so very wrong.

I grabbed her, unable to keep even an inch of space between us. Needing to hold her and remind myself that she'd made it through that day. That she was still here—still breathing, still alive. That the world could keep spinning simply because her heart beat on.

"You could have told me," I said as I dragged her into my lap and curled my body around hers. Protecting her. Trying to be a shield against anything that might hurt her, though I was too late. The pain came from inside, and there was nothing I could do to stop it.

Anabeth shook her head, sighing and collapsing against me. "I hated myself for everything. I hated myself so much."

"I meant, from the start. You could have told me about the drugs—I would have helped you get clean. I would have beat the shit out of Finn for even bringing that stuff around you."

"It wasn't his fault. I've blamed him for so long, but it was my choice to use." She clung to me, fisting her hands in my shirt. "I didn't think of it as a problem, though. We used, we didn't—there was never a need, you know? It never seemed like a big deal. Not until that day." She shook her head. "I'm so sorry I didn't say anything about Finn when he started using. I never thought he'd fall so deep."

I couldn't think about my brother right then. Not without a lot of fucking anger. He should have protected Anabeth, not led her down the path he did. And knowing what had happened to him— the years of addiction, the years in prison—it could have all been her. I could have lost her forever. I was pissed enough to want to hunt him down and beat the piss out of him, but I didn't. Couldn't. Anabeth was a mess and still needed me, and this time, I wouldn't fail her.

I would push her, instead. I would get the full story. "Tell me about Vegas."

Anabeth took a deep breath as if steeling herself against more pain. Fuck, I hated that this hurt her so much.

"Miss moved me there to get me away from Finn, though she'd thought it would be temporary. Paul, the man who opened the door when you came looking for me, was a friend of hers. He was supposed to put me up while I got clean and earned my GED since there was no way I was going back to school here."

"But you stayed. So what happened?"

"Paul was a medium on the Strip—talking to dead people and charming tourists. That's how he knew Miss—the two met at some new-age gifted seminar thing. Anyway, he took me with him once or twice while he performed, just to get me out of the apartment. I fell in love with what he did, with the people watching him and the way he commanded the crowds. I wanted it for myself, but Miss didn't want me on stage. She didn't feel I was ready for a world so dirty and dishonest. Paul agreed and honored her request. For a while."

"What changed his mind?"

"I kept slipping up—using. Relapsing, I guess, though I'd never really been clean to start with, so maybe that word doesn't fit. Whatever—I would go out, get high, get into trouble. Paul made me go to school to get my GED and even put me through a vocational program to be a dental hygienist, all while I—"

My chuckle stopped her. "Sorry. It's just—"

"Can't see me dealing with teeth all day?"

"Not at all."

"Yeah, I couldn't either. And I was so miserable and depressed, which just made me chase the drugs even more. It was a vicious cycle, but the one thing that made me happy—made me think there was some sort of future to look forward to—was hanging out at Paul's shows and watching the different performers. Knowing I had enough skills with the tarot deck to do the same thing. Finally, Paul offered me a chance—he'd put me on the stage with him and get me started in paranormal entertainment, but only if I stayed clean."

Smart guy. "So you quit."

"Yeah. I quit. Haven't touched anything harsher than an aspirin since."

I kissed the top of her head, so damn grateful for the guy I'd hated for so long. Without him, I could have truly lost her. I would never be able to pay him back for what he did for Anabeth.

And I'd never get over how she'd pulled herself up practically all alone to get what she wanted and to do it without drugs in her path.

"I'm proud of you."

"Don't be," she said, sitting back and pulling away to wipe her face. "I never should have used in the first place. I never should have lied to everyone about all of it." She looked up at me with so much sadness in her eyes. I couldn't resist. I cupped her face, my big hands sliding all the way into her hairline.

"I hate that you went through all this alone."

"I had Miss—she called every day and did her best to be there when I really needed her to be."

Which we both knew wasn't enough. I wouldn't speak ill of the woman for doing what she had thought was best, but that didn't mean her actions hadn't caused me pain. Hadn't helped ruin the last fourteen years of my life.

I'd just have to learn to swallow down that anger at some point. "I came to see her—we had dinner right here in this kitchen numerous times. All these years, and she never said a word to me."

"She hated keeping my seizure and the baby a secret, but I made her promise. I begged her every time I called. I couldn't deal with you knowing... And the thought that you'd hate me for what I did? It all just hurt so much. The pain never stopped for a second."

I rubbed her back and kissed her again when it didn't seem as if she could go on, this time on her reddened cheek. The one without the bruise marring it. Jesus, I had so much to make up for. I'd failed her so hard.

I wouldn't ever fail her again.

"It's over now, Firefly." I wrapped my arms around her and pulled her against me, wanting to protect her. To hold on to her. To keep her safe. To keep her mine. "I've got you, and I'm not letting you go. No matter what."

She shook her head, so fucking stubborn as always. "You should. You should push me away and make me leave. Bishop, I—"

"Stop beating yourself up," I said, speaking every word with distinction. "You died that day. I could have lost you."

Her eyes looked so pained, so heartbreakingly sad when she stared up at me. "I lost our baby."

Yeah, that hurt. A lot. More than I'd ever thought possible, really. The idea that we'd created a life, a child, and that drugs had destroyed the tiny being before it had even really begun... I didn't know how to deal with that. Didn't know how to grieve the loss of possibility so many years later.

What I did know was that I'd give anything to try again. "You called it her earlier. Would we have had a girl?"

"I don't know. They never told me one way or the other, but I think of her as a little girl. I always think of her."

I had a feeling I would too, now. "I wish you would have told me so I could mourn with you. I could have held you up when you fell, beautiful."

She sniffed, resting her forehead against my chest as I rocked her. "I was so afraid you'd hate me."

"Maybe I should." I held her tighter when she tried to pull away. "You took my choices away from me and cut me out of everything I would have wanted to do—taking care of you, mourning our loss together, growing into adults who could have better dealt with all that shit. You stole that from me."

Her breathing sped up, and she choked on a quiet, "I'm so sorry."

"So am I, and it's going to take some time for me to come to grips with this. But I *will* come to grips with it. And I need you to know that I'm still all in, Anabeth. Always have been, always will be." I held her tighter, unable to let go. Not willing to give her a chance to pull away again but needing to know one more thing. The most important thing. "So what do I need to do to make sure you're all in with me?"

She jerked back, staring at me with wide eyes. "What do you mean?"

Cards on the table time. "You and me. Together. How do we do this? Do you need to go back to Vegas to perform?"

She nodded slowly, still watching me. Still stunned. That was okay, I was stunning myself pretty damn good, too.

"When?"

"I can push a few things, but I have a show next week that I can't miss."

More time than I'd thought. But only if she wanted to share those days with me. "How long do you want to stay here, then?"

"Bishop, this is cra—"

"Do you want to be with me, Anabeth?"

She sat as still as a stone, watching me with bloodshot eyes. Taking me in. I refused to waver, holding her stare like a man on a mission. Like a man about to give his heart away one last time.

"Do you?" I prodded when she didn't answer me. Impatient. I'd waited so long for this moment—I was tired of fucking waiting.

Her nod had my heart soaring, and her whispered yes nearly killed me. Finally. No fucking way was I letting her walk away again. Not ever. No matter what, I'd be by her side from that day forward.

"Good, because I want to be with you too. So fucking much, Anabeth. I don't want to waste another second without you right beside me. That means we deal with your career and my responsibilities here together. As a team."

She nodded again, still looking completely surprised. "You want to *be* with me."

"I always have, Firefly." I yanked her close and captured her mouth with mine, unable to resist those soft, sweet lips another second. Not wanting to ever stop kissing her. And when she moaned softly for me, when she opened her mouth against mine, I took full advantage. Licking my way inside and tasting every inch of her mouth. Gripping her hips and holding her tight against me until it felt as if we could heal ourselves through that kiss alone. That we could put the pieces back together.

"So much lost time," I said as I released her mouth so I could nibble down her neck. "So many missed opportunities to taste you."

"Bishop."

Hands on her ass, I pulled her closer, wanting to hang on forever. Never wanting to let go. "Just keep saying my name, Firefly. Every time you do, I know we're one step closer to forever."

She smiled, shifting around and pulling up one leg to straddle me before leaning in to place the softest, sweetest kiss of my life on my lips. And when she pulled away, when she moved back to give me the real smile of hers that people so rarely saw, I knew she was mine. Forever.

My heart felt so damned full, but there were still things that had to be said. "You and me? We're going to work. Nothing can stand in our way anymore. But we have to be honest with each other. No more secrets. No hiding from anything. We have to be each other's biggest ally. I don't want any doubt between us."

"No more doubt." She kissed me again, her lips so fucking soft against mine. Her body so warm and pliant. "Bishop."

"See, Firefly? You said my name...that's one step closer."

She laughed and rolled her hips, teasing me right there at her kitchen table. Offering all of herself to me. And I took. Tasted. Devoured. Because she was mine and I was hers, and nothing—not drugs, not the past, not a couple of jobs we both loved—would ever take her away from me again.

I'd make damn sure of it.

Chapter Twenty-Four

BISHOP

Four days. It took us four days to come up for air after making a commitment to each other. I'd moved Anabeth into my place, accepting the offers of my brothers and friends to guard the house...so long as they stayed outside. Gage and Rex had moved into the house on the ridge so he could fix the two broken doors and give us some space. Anabeth and I had a lot of reconnecting to do, and that required privacy. Something the guys and Gage accepted. I had a feeling I'd be mocked relentlessly once I went back to work, though.

Worth it.

I opened the door to The Baker's Cottage, guiding Anabeth through the opening with my hand on her lower back. And if I dropped that hand just a little to brush across her ass, so be it. She definitely didn't seem to mind. In fact, she shot me a saucy smile over her shoulder before Shye stole her attention.

"Good to see you, Anabeth. Bishop." The little blonde grinned while escorting us to a table by the bar, probably having heard all about our renewed relationship from Alder. My brother was a nosy fucker at times. He claimed he needed to know what was going on to be able to keep the town safe. I figured he just liked to gossip.

"The soup of the day is corn chowder, and Katie's got a meatloaf on special that's real popular. Can I get you both something to drink while you look over the menus?"

Before we could answer, Alder came strolling through the door from the kitchen with Katie following him. Gage wasn't far behind, which didn't surprise me. Finn walking through the front door at basically the same time certainly did, though.

Anabeth stiffened at my side, and all that unresolved anger from her story—from learning he'd used drugs with her, introduced them to her knowing she was the child of an addict, and never said a goddamned word to me about it—overflowed. I had thought the next time I saw Finn, I'd beat his ass. I felt more like I was going to kill him.

"Bishop, please." Anabeth leaned close, her hand on my face and her eyes holding mine. "It's the past. Don't take things out on Finn."

"Why do you think I'm going to take anything out on him?"

She raised an eyebrow. "If looks could kill, he'd be toast right now."

So I hadn't lost my SEAL glare. "Good."

Anabeth sat back as Finn headed for the bar, nodding in our direction but not saying anything. Which was fine by me. I had no idea what would come out of my mouth if I dared to try to speak to him in that moment.

Gage and Katie seemed to be having a conversation at the far side of the bar from where Finn sat down. And by seemed to, I meant Katie looked to be babbling endlessly while Gage stood there and watched her. Other people might have thought he appeared bored or uninterested because his face looked blank, but there was a carefulness to the stoic expression and a fire in his eyes. He was anything but bored, though I had no idea if Katie could discern his interest. If the way she headed toward Finn as soon as she noticed him, practically leaving Gage behind in mid-sentence, was any indication, that would be a no.

Alder sat down across from us, grabbing Shye and pulling her into his lap. "Been wondering when we'd see you two again."

I pulled Anabeth's chair closer and sat back, looping my arm behind her. "I seem to remember you disappearing for a few days after the lovely Shye finally stopped running away from you."

"I never ran," Shye said, smiling at my brother in a way that he had damn well better be thankful for. Any man would want their woman to look at them like that. "I just never realized he was chasing me."

Alder grinned and pulled her in for a small kiss before refocusing on us. "This is going to sound weird, but you two smell like spearmint."

I grinned as Anabeth blushed a little. Yeah, we had a bit of an obsession. Anabeth had admitted her addiction to the taste was brought on by memories of me, so I fueled that. Spearmint gum, candies, her teas...I made sure she had all of it around her.

And the fact that she had a tendency to straddle my lap and kiss me nice and deep and long whenever I chewed spearmint gum certainly helped.

I pulled out a piece and shot my girl a wink. "It's just gum, man. No big deal."

"That's some strong gum." He sat back, looking me over, flicking a glance to Anabeth before asking me, "What do I need to know?"

I shrugged, rubbing my thumb against Anabeth's shoulder

when I felt her stiffen beside me. "We're together. What more do you want?"

Alder eyed Anabeth, a wary sort of expression on his face. I knew what he was thinking—he'd been the one to drag my ass out of Vegas after Anabeth had left. He'd seen me deeper into a bottle than I'd ever been in my life and ready to give up everything because of how badly she'd hurt me. He didn't know the whys of what had happened, only the results, and as a big brother, he probably had concerns. I understood that. I'd still fight my own brother if he dared to speak against her.

But Alder had been a happy fucker since Shye had finally become his. No longer grumpy, the man sat a little deeper, gripped his woman a little tighter, and fucking smiled.

"Well then, welcome home, Anabeth. It's good to have you back."

Anabeth rested her head on my shoulder and laid her hand on my thigh. "It's good to be home."

Thank fuck for that, because having her home was about the best thing I could have ever imagined. Even as short-lived as it would be.

"We should celebrate." Alder smiled at Shye. "What does Katie have that we can toast with?"

"No alcohol," Anabeth and I said at the same time, both chuckling afterward. Yeah, she didn't drink, which meant I probably wouldn't anymore either. I was okay with that choice too. Whatever it took to keep her happy, sober, and by my side, I'd do.

Shye gave us a questioning sort of smile. "Toast but no alcohol. Got it. I think there's a bottle or two of that sparkling grape juice we had for the kids during the grand opening. Would that work?"

Alder raised his eyebrows at us, looking back to Shye when we nodded. "Sounds good, honey. Make sure you grab a glass for yourself."

Shye rushed off, stopping at the bar where Gage, Katie, and Finn sat. As she spoke to them, she nodded toward us, and my gut locked down. Fuck me, she was going to send them over to celebrate with us. Had I not known about Finn's involvement in Anabeth's almost death, I would have been happy to spend time with my girl and my friends and family together. Now?

No fucking way.

"Stop," Anabeth whispered, angling her body across mine so she could whisper in my ear. "Nothing was his fault, and I made him swear never to tell you about the drugs. He didn't know about... anything else."

The baby. He hadn't known about the baby. Didn't matter, though. He knew she was using, and he never said a fucking word.

Anabeth tried to pull away, but my hand gripping her waist stopped her. I stared into those blue eyes that meant the world to me, the ones I'd missed for a damn long time. The ones I swore I'd wake up to every day for the rest of our lives.

"He put you in danger. I will never forgive him for that."

"Bishop, don't—"

"Hey, guys," Finn said as he appeared beside the table. "I hear you've got some news."

I tried to control my temper—I tried real fucking hard. I purposely thought about Finn's own fight with addiction, about the phone call I'd received while stationed in Afghanistan that he'd been arrested for dealing, about the years he'd lost being sent to prison for a crime he hadn't committed. I tried to keep all of that in the front of my mind.

But then he fucked up.

"Good to see you, Anabeth," Finn said, and he dropped his hand onto her shoulder. Anabeth jerked, her face going pale and her body leaning into mine as if on instinct. That obvious discomfort, that fear, snapped my fucking leash.

"Don't touch her," I said as I rose to my feet. Anabeth tried to hold onto my arm, but I simply squeezed her hand and kept going. Refusing to take my eyes off Finn. "I know what you did, so don't you dare lay a finger on her. Don't even fucking look at her."

Finn's eyes went wide. "Bishop, I'm sorry. I never thought—"

"No. You don't get to be sorry right now. You don't get to seek forgiveness or try to smooth this over."

"What's going on here?" Alder moved between us, looking ready to tear the two of us apart if need be.

But I didn't need to tear into Finn physically. Not yet, at least. "Finn here and his drug use reared its ugly head again."

Alder's expression turned thunderous. "You're using?"

"No. Fuck no." Finn took a step back and ran a hand through his hair. "I... Back when I was using and Anabeth was still here—"

"He used with her," I said, interrupting him and refusing to let him spin the story. "He almost killed her."

"Why did we not know this?" Alder said, looking from Finn to Anabeth with a stormy expression on his face.

Anabeth grabbed my arm, sliding her body against mine. Effectively putting herself between Finn and me, something that just revved my temper even more.

"I made him swear never to tell." She pushed against me, trying to take my focus off my brother. Trying to calm me. "This isn't Finn's fault, Bishop. I have to take responsibility for my actions."

"You got scared when he touched you."

"I felt uncomfortable because I still associate Finn with...what I lost. I'm not scared of him, though. And I don't want you fighting with him because of what happened so long ago." She rose onto the balls of her feet and tugged my chin until I looked down at her. "Please. Let this go so we can move forward."

This girl. How could I refuse her anything? But I needed to make a point.

Still, I never wanted Anabeth to be unhappy, so I nodded, and I leaned down to give her a kiss when she smiled. Then I gently pushed her out of the way before I swung and slammed my fist into Finn's mouth. I'd never heard such a satisfying crack in all my life.

Anabeth screamed, and the room exploded into motion.

"Jesus, Bishop," Alder yelled as he lunged for Finn. Gage grabbed me from behind, tugging me back. Glaring at Finn as if ready to jump into the fight on my side. Right or wrong, I knew Gage would be with me, but I wasn't looking to brawl. Not really. I'd just given my little brother a taste of what he'd deserved.

"One," I said, pointing at Finn who had Alder holding his arms the same way Gage held mine. "You deserve that one for what you did, but it'll be the only one for the past. You bring any of that shit back around her, you threaten her sobriety in any way, and I won't stop at just one."

Finn glared at me but nodded, wiping the blood from his lip. "Fine. Good luck to you both."

He yanked his arms away from Alder and headed for the door, looking pissed as hell. Good. Let him be mad. I had fourteen years of *mad* to deal with—he could take a little on himself.

I pulled away from Gage and watched my brother leave. Waited for him to disappear around the corner of the building. Waited to make sure he wasn't coming back.

"You really think that was a good idea?" Alder asked, looking ready to spit nails.

"Yeah, I do."

He nodded, glancing from Anabeth to me. "This isn't going to be a long-term thing, is it? This beef with Finn?"

I tugged my girl back into my side, hanging on tight. Keeping her safe. "No. Like I said, he deserved the one. I won't bring it back up so long as he doesn't upset Anabeth."

Alder didn't look convinced, but that was too fucking bad. I had my girl, I had a future before me that I'd never thought possible, and there was no way I was letting Finn fuck that up.

"Fine. Just don't push him too hard. I don't want to see anyone travel back down a road to addiction." Alder shook his head and walked away, grabbing Shye as he passed her and tugging her with him. There was a protective vibe about the way he held her, an aura of danger. I had a feeling Finn wouldn't be acting as Shye's guard for a while.

"Nice boots." Gage bumped his shoulder into mine, watching Alder walk away. "Nice punch, too."

"Stupid punch," Anabeth said, grabbing my hand and looking at my knuckles. "Did you hurt yourself?"

As if I'd ever admit something like that. Besides, sore knuckles were worth it. "Not a bit."

Gage snorted. "I think it's time for me to get to work." He nodded at Anabeth. "You keep him under control for me, okay?"

Her body went stiff, but the entertainer in her kicked in quick, her stage smile lifting her lips easily. "I'll do my best."

Jackasses, the both of them. "Go. I'm spending the day with my woman."

"Never thought I'd hear you say those words, man." Gage laughed as he headed for the door, leaving Anabeth and me standing together in the entryway of the restaurant. She turned to face me, not looking all that thrilled. *Uh oh.*

"You know that was stupid, right?"

I shrugged. I didn't think it was stupid, but I wasn't going to fight her on that. "You know I'd do anything to keep you safe, right?"

"That's not the point—"

"I love you, Anabeth." My heart nearly exploded when her eyes went wide and her hands gripped me tighter. "In the spirit of no secrets and no hiding things from one another, I need to tell you that. I love you, I always have, and I always will. No one gets to make you feel uncomfortable when I'm around. Whether that person is family or not. I will always fight for you."

"Bishop, I—"

"Unless you're about to say I love you back to me, don't. You won't change my mind on this. You are my heart, Firefly. Let me take care of you."

She stood there staring up at me for what felt like hours. Days. Fuck, maybe even years. Luckily, I had patience. I waited her out, giving her time to get her words together. To find her own truth inside herself. And when a bright, soft, real smile spread across her face, I knew I'd been right to wait.

"I love you too, you big oaf. Now give me a kiss so we can go back and toast with Alder and Shye."

Good thing I had experience following orders. "Yes, ma'am."

I kissed her, and I grabbed her ass and tugged her against my aching cock just because I could. Because I knew she'd like it. She moaned, opening her lips to me and sliding her tongue against mine. So needy, this girl. So perfect. So mine.

Forever this time.

Epilogue
TWO MONTHS LATER

ANABETH

If you don't stop looking at me like you're about to devour me, I'll never finish stripping off this stage makeup."

Bishop's sexy smile didn't ease up for a second. "I do so love to watch you strip, Firefly. Nothing new there."

No, nothing new at all. Bishop and I had spent a good week in Justice after the incident at my house. Incident—because that was how I reconciled someone's death at Bishop's hands. The man who'd come barging in, who'd tossed me to the floor and held me hostage, could have easily killed me and likely would have. Bishop had defended me and taken care of the problem in the quickest, most concise way possible. I refused to see anything wrong with that.

After that day, we'd spent all our time together. Lots of hours alone, in bed, at the kitchen table. Hours of talking, buckets of tears from me and maybe even some from him, though I'd never tell anyone that. He wouldn't either. We had a rule to tell each other everything, so his secrets were safe *with* me.

And when my time had been up, when I'd needed to return to Vegas for booked dates, he'd come with me. We'd had to separate a few times over the last two months—usually because he was needed back in Justice for something to do with the Soul Suckers or the flooding that had destroyed three houses along with Bishop's truck. Those times were hard—long distance sucked, but we made the best of it. Chatting, texting, video calls—we never went more than a couple of hours without being in touch. And when we got back together? When he walked off a plane in Vegas or I drove into Justice? Explosive. We couldn't keep our hands off one another, which had led to another blessing in our crazy story.

I was pregnant.

I'd known when we'd reconnected that Bishop not wearing a condom was a bad idea, but I hadn't addressed it with him. I hadn't wanted to. Maybe deep down, I'd craved that link to him—the permanency of a child together. Or maybe I'd simply not wanted anything between us after so long apart. I don't know for sure where my head had been at, but we'd been blessed with a second chance to have a family, and this time, I wouldn't screw anything up. This time, I'd get to tell him about the baby. Soon. Real soon.

I finally wiped away the last of the makeup that made me look just a little younger under all those lights. As I threw away the tissue, my tarot deck caught my attention. The urge to pull one card, to peek at the future, was one I couldn't resist. So I spread the cards out a bit, and I took my time choosing one. The right one.

I hadn't pulled the three of swords since I'd told Bishop why I'd left Justice. The streak lived on.

Bishop's warm, smooth voice wrapped around me as he asked, "What card is it tonight?"

"The empress." I ran a finger over the face on the card, smiling. "It means femininity and beauty—"

"Definitely the right card for you tonight."

It also meant other things, like nature and abundance. Like fertility.

"I think you're right," I said. "Definitely the right card."

I stood, heading for the rack of clothes in the corner. Bishop stopped me, though. Grabbing me around the hips and yanking me down into his lap.

"You're beautiful, Firefly, but you seem anxious," he said as he nuzzled my neck. "Talk to me."

Anxious was an understatement. Excited, terrified, elated, worried...all better descriptors. I should have known he'd recognize that I had something going on. The man might as well have been psychic when it came to me, always searching, investigating, watching. Always striving to keep me happy. To keep me with him. He had no idea how much it would take to tear me away, a fact I'd need to remedy. Soon. But first, I had a surprise for him.

"I wanted to wait until we got back to my place," I said as I ran a hand over the muscles in his shoulder. So tense—the man must have been worried about bad news.

"Now," he said, not giving me an option to hide anymore. "No secrets and no hiding. Tell me now."

Our rules, laid out for me. A good reminder. I ran my fingers through his hair, staring into those gray eyes I loved so much. "I want to put my condo up for sale."

He frowned. "Okay."

"And I want to move back to Justice. For good."

His frown only deepened. "But you love being on stage."

"I do. I love reading tarot cards and entertaining tourists. But I love you more." I leaned in to kiss him, my nerves firing in rapid succession and making my hands shake as I braced myself against his chest. Readied myself for the real news. "And I think I'm going to love being a mom most of all."

Bishop froze, stiff and unyielding beneath me. "Anabeth—"

The awe in his voice, the excitement...it made me grin. Made me lean in as I nodded. "I'm pregnant."

His arms wrapped around me and tugged me closer, his lips finding mine and claiming ownership. Deep, slow kisses led to wandering hands and clothes pushed aside. Led to him holding me up as I straddled his hips, led to him thrusting deep inside me as he chanted my name.

And when we were done—sated and sweaty and still wrapped around one another—he finally spoke.

"Are you sure?"

"Positive. I went to the doctor this morning before picking you up at the airport. I wanted to make sure the tests I took at home were accurate."

His hands moved to my stomach, holding me. Holding us. "A baby."

"Our baby."

"And you want this?" he asked, looking up at me with so much hope in his eyes. "Me, the baby, to come home to Justice... Because I won't make you. You can keep working here, and we'll figure things out. Whatever makes you happy."

My silly man. "*You* make me happy. Being away from you hurts too much, and this place isn't where I want to be anymore." I kissed him again. And again. Only pulling away when those kisses were about to turn into more. Not because I didn't want him, but because I still had things to say. "You're my home, Bishop. I want to be where you are, and I want the quiet, small-town life Justice will give us so we can raise our family."

His grip tightened on my hips. "We still have trouble with the Soul Suckers. It's not as safe as when we were kids."

"Will you let them near me?" I dragged his hand over onto my belly, pressing it against where someday soon, a child would make it swell. "Would you ever let them near us?"

His eyes hardened in an instant, and his voice turned rough. Mean. SEAL Bishop showing his face. "Not in a million fucking years."

"Then I'm not worried about them. I just want you and our baby—I want a family. And I want that in Justice."

Bishop sighed, pulling me close for another sweet kiss before resting his forehead against mine. "I love you, Firefly, and I'll do everything I can to make you happy. To keep our family together and safe. I promise you that."

"I know you will, which is why this isn't a hard decision for me." I pulled his face closer and pressed my lips to his before sitting back with a smile. "So how about we go back to my condo and you make me extra happy. We should really make sure we've christened every room before I sell the place."

"I don't know. Shouldn't you be resting? You're in a fragile state." His grin belied his words, though. As did the way his hands kept roaming over my bare skin, sliding under the silk dressing gown that hung from my shoulders.

"True. We probably should take it easy." I bit back a laugh when his smile fell. Two could play his game. "I mean, if you don't want to slide that thick, hard cock inside me again…"

I trailed off as I teased him, running my fingertips over the tip of his erection where it sat wedged between us. He jerked and hummed, pulling me closer. Nuzzling my neck before placing a hard bite there.

"I always want to be buried inside your sweet pussy, my little tease. It's my favorite place to be. My heaven."

"Then let's go home. We can celebrate."

Bishop smacked my ass lightly, giving me a stern frown. "No business calls or interruptions."

Yeah, I was bad about that. My industry tended to keep weird hours, and my constant connection to my phone while in Vegas was something he wasn't the biggest fan of. But tonight would be ours. "Just you, me, and a lot of hours being naked together. Promise."

"I like the way you think." He helped me stand, tucking himself away before refastening his pants when he stood up. And then he was on me, holding me tight, cupping my face in his hands as if I was something precious to him. As if he couldn't stay away. "This is a gift, Firefly. You, me, the baby, moving back to Justice. All of it is such a dream come true. One I promise not to take for granted."

My heart melted, tears coming fast and hard to my eyes. "I know."

"I'll protect you both. Come hell or high water, no one will get near you. I'll blow the whole damn town apart before that happens."

"I know that too."

And I did. Which was why I felt safe returning to Justice.

"The Kennards would never allow a family member to be hurt," Bishop said, holding me tight. "I want you to be my family."

"I am. We will be."

"No, not just because of the baby. I've waited fourteen years to give you this. I don't want to waste another second." He reached into his suit coat pocket and pulled out a little black box before dropping to one knee. "Marry me, Anabeth Monroe. Marry me, and let's be a family together."

Every wish, every dream I'd ever had, was coming true. Somehow, I'd earned a second chance at the life I'd always wanted, and I would never take that for granted. So I nodded, unable not to tell the man I'd loved for over half my life yes. Chanting the word in a whisper barely loud enough for me to hear, let alone Bishop. But I didn't need to worry about that. He knew. He knew, and he took control as he always did. He slid the square solitaire ring onto my finger, placed a gentle kiss against my bare belly, and rose to his feet, wiping away my happy tears before tugging my dressing gown off.

"Drive-thru chapel's open. Get dressed, and let's go get this done."

"Now? You want to get married *right now*? Just us?"

"I lost you once, lost a chance at a family too. I won't go through that again." He palmed my belly, holding my gaze with those steely gray eyes I wanted to wake up to every single day for the rest of my life. "I love you, and I want you tied to me in a legal way—with ink and big capital letters that say you're mine. So be mine, Firefly. Right now. Forever."

How could I possibly say no to that?

"Yes."

Acknowledgments

I finished final edits on this book while staying at a million-dollar loft in Chicago with some priceless friends. To all my BGW girls... thank you. For the laughs, the support, the kind words, the face masks, the treats, the coffee runs, and the love you share with me. Will Smith said to surround yourself with people who fan your flames instead of smothering them. Burn bright, ladies.

With every book, Lisa Hollett with Silently Correcting Your Grammar has to balance making sure my words are ready for the shelf and keeping me from crying over a shitty draft. It's a rough job, and I'm always so very grateful that she invests the time with me. Thank you, friend. Enjoy some crackers out of your beetle kill pine bowl.

Franci Neill read this book to help me find those final mistakes every manuscript has while on a cruise in way warmer weather than I suffered through while writing it. Thanks for taking Anabeth and Bishop along to paradise!

Finally, and most importantly, to my girls. May your hearts be filled with love, your life filled with laughs, and your arms filled with hugs. I love you both without end.